"Look around," Joe said. "Remember where everyone is."

"Why?" John Hancock asked.

Joe began to make notes in his notebook. "Because," he told the young photographer, "that's how we're going to solve this murder—before anyone else does. Right?"

"Right," John said. He snapped a quick photo of the scene.

Joe looked around uncertainly. Sam and David gazed up and down the car. Joe had a sudden thought. The original plan was for them to work on this  murder case as a team. But maybe that wasn't going to happen.

What if Sam, or David, or even John *couldn't* be part of the team?

What if one of them was the murderer? . . .

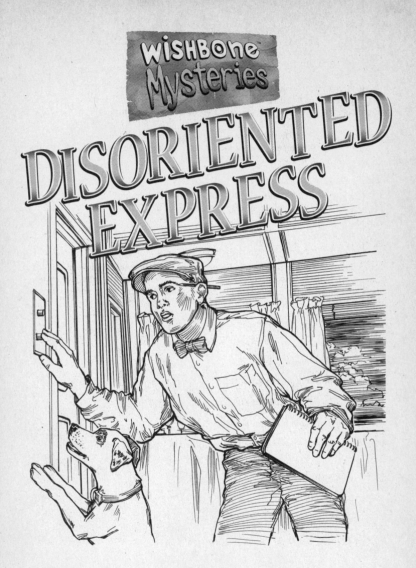

WISHBONE Mysteries

DISORIENTED EXPRESS

by **Brad Strickland and Thomas E. Fuller**

WISHBONE™ created by Rick Duffield

Big Red Chair Books™, *A Division of **Lyrick Publishing**™*

This book is a work of fiction. The characters, incidents, and dialogues are products of the authors' imagination and are not to be construed as real. Any resemblance to actual events or persons, living or dead, is entirely coincidental.

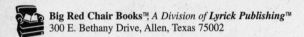 **Big Red Chair Books**™, *A Division of **Lyrick Publishing***™
300 E. Bethany Drive, Allen, Texas 75002

©1998 Big Feats! Entertainment

Edited by Kevin Ryan

Copy edited by Jonathon Brodman

Cover concept and design by Lyle Miller

Interior illustrations by Kathryn Yingling

Wishbone photograph by Carol Kaelson

Cover train photo courtesy of The B&O Railroad Museum Collection

Library of Congress Catalog Card Number: 98-84969

ISBN: 1-57064-502-7

First printing: December 1998

10 9 8 7 6 5 4 3 2 1

Printed in the United States of America

For my father and mother, who taught me
to love the adventure of reading
—Brad Strickland

This book is dedicated to the memory of my father,
Roy T. Fuller. Thanks for everything, Dad.
—Thomas E. Fuller

Cast of Characters

THE PLAYERS	THEIR ROLES
DAVID BARNES. . . . . *Joe's neighbor and friend*	JOHN KINDLER scientist
MARGARET BRADBURY. . . . . . . *runs the Windom Foundation*	VANESSA STEELE actress
HENRY COOPER. . . . . *museum director and train buff*	HENRY COOPER conductor
TRAVIS DEL RIO . . . . *sporting goods store-owner (Don't chew his catchers' mitts!)*	LEW BLACK private detective
WANDA GILMORE . . . . *Joe's neighbor (Her garden's great for digging!)*	NOREEN "NOSY" NORDECKER gossip columnist
KILGORE GURNEY. . . . . *bookstore owner and Joe's former employer*	DR. MORTIMER STITCHER medical doctor
JOHN HANCOCK. . . . . *Joe's visitor from California, and son of Ellen's good friend*	ELVIN MORSE newspaper photographer
SAMANTHA KEPLER. . . . . *Joe's friend and Wishbone's ear-scratcher*	LADY VICTORIA KINCADE diamond heiress
WALTER KEPLER . . . . *Sam's dad (He smells like pizza!)*	COLONEL RICHARD ABERDEEN Lady Victoria's guardian

THE PLAYERS	THEIR ROLES
MADDY KINGSTON.......... *computer expert at Oakdale College Natural History Museum*	SYLVIA CARMICHAEL nightclub singer
MICHAEL PATTERSON *Monica's twin brother, and co-owner of Mystery Murders, Inc.*	
MONICA PATTERSON *Michael's twin sister, and co-owner of Mystery Murders, Inc.*	
BOB PRUITT .... *Joe, Sam, and David's former English teacher*	LASLO CARBINE arms dealer and spy
QUENTIN QUARREL .... *retired college professor*	PROFESSOR ZEBULON DIRE archeologist
ELLEN TALBOT............. *Joe's mom and Wishbone's chef*	MARJORY MACBRIDE best-selling novelist
JOE TALBOT .... *Wishbone's best friend*	MICHAEL O'HARA cub reporter
WISHBONE................ *our favorite Jack Russell terrier*	BORSHOI pedigreed Russian wolfhound
HORACE ZIMMERMAN .... *friend of Wanda Gilmore, businessman, and old-car collector*	COUNT PETROV ZORSKY art collector

FROM THE BIG RED CHAIR . . .

Oh . . . hi! Wishbone here. You caught me right in the middle of some of my favorite things—books. Let me welcome you to the WISHBONE MYSTERIES. In each story, I help my human friends solve a puzzling mystery. In *DISORIENTED EXPRESS*, my pals Joe, Sam, David, and our special guest, John Hancock, and I ride on a train to take part in a game—a murder-mystery game. During the trip, Joe finds out that a *real* spy story is connected to the train. . . .

The story takes place early in the spring, during the same time period as the events that you'll see in the second season of my WISHBONE television show. In this story, Joe is fourteen, and he and his friends are in the eighth grade. Like me, they are always ready for adventure . . . and a good mystery.

You're in for a real treat, so pull up a chair and a snack and sink your teeth into *DISORIENTED EXPRESS!*

Chapter One

"A train?" Wishbone's ears shot up with excitement. "We're going on a *train ride*? Wow!"

"A train?" asked their nine-year-old house guest, John Hancock.

Joe Talbot grinned at the brown-haired boy. "That's right, John," he said. "It's a special trip. I'm really glad that you're going to be able to go along with us." When Wishbone pawed at Joe's leg, the boy laughed and bent to pat the excited white-with-brown-and-black-spots Jack Russell terrier. "And I'm glad you'll be going along with us, too, buddy."

Ellen Talbot, Joe's mom, smiled. She, John, Joe, and Wishbone were in the kitchen. They had just finished breakfast. Ellen took a last sip of coffee and said, "That's right. We'll leave the Oakdale train station at five this evening, ride all the way to Zenith, and then we'll come back home on Sunday. I hope you won't mind spending two days that way!"

John smiled. John's mom and Joe's mom had been good friends when they were younger. Now,

John's family lived in northern California, but he was visiting Oakdale over spring break. Wishbone liked John a lot, and he thought John was enjoying his visit to the Talbots' town. Wishbone wagged his tail. "Say you don't mind, John!"

As if John had been listening to the dog, he said, "I don't mind at all. Mrs. Talbot, are you sure Wishbone will be allowed on the train?"

Wishbone gave Ellen a begging look. "What! I might not be allowed on the train? Please say it isn't so, Ellen! It's Friday, and I don't want to be alone all weekend! How will I open my kibble? Who'll play with me? Oh, please, please, please, please!"

"Of course, John, we can take Wishbone," Ellen said. "In fact, Wanda Gilmore, our next-door neighbor, is involved in planning this train trip and personally invited him to come along."

Wishbone barked happily. "Thank you! And I'll thank Wanda, too—and then I'll bury a nice bone in her garden!"

Joe grinned and said, "Mom, maybe you'd better explain to John how this train ride is really part of a game."

"All right," Ellen replied. "John, as Joe said, this is a special train ride. A murder is going to take place on the train!"

"*What?*" John asked, sounding shocked.

With a chuckle, Ellen said, "I don't mean a real murder. It's only a make-believe one. It's part of a mystery game. Everyone will have a part to play in the game—it's a grown-up kind of 'let's pretend.' It will be just like one of the great murder mysteries Joe likes to read. The passengers will try to gather clues to solve

10

the murder. The first one to crack the case will win a prize."

"A prize!" Wishbone twirled around and around. "A prize! I love prizes! Oh, I want to be the detective who wins the prize!"

"That sounds like a lot of fun," John said.

"We'll have a great time," Joe said. "The hard part will be pretending it's the 1930s. That's when the murder-mystery game is supposed to take place."

"That's right," Ellen added. "A few weeks ago, Wanda asked me to help her find books on clothing styles from the 1930s. We did a lot of research at the library, and we came up with some great ideas. We passed along the information to the people who are organizing the train trip. We'll all wear costumes— except maybe Wishbone."

Wishbone sniffed. "Who ever heard of a dog wearing a costume? That's just silly! Anyway, I'm very handsome even when I'm not wearing a thing!"

"I'll introduce you to my two best friends, Sam and David," Joe said to John. "They're coming along, too. The three of us are planning to work together to solve the mystery."

Ellen smiled. "Just remember—this is the kind of mystery in which anyone and everyone is a possible suspect." She reached into her purse on the kitchen table and handed a printed page to Joe. "Here. This explains all about it."

Joe held the paper so that John and Wishbone could see it. The three of them gathered around closely to get a good look. The flyer had a big picture of a steam locomotive on it. The train engine looked old, but in very good condition. The engine was all smooth, sleek curves. It was painted a shiny silvery-gray on the sides and what looked like the front bumper of the train. The rounded metal cowling covering the engine was painted yellow. Wishbone blinked when he saw all the wheels. On the side of the train he could see, there were two small wheels up front, then three huge wheels, and finally two small wheels at the back.

Joe read aloud from the flyer: "'The *Zenith Condor* was built in 1935. It has always been kept in first-class condition. Its run to Zenith will begin at five P.M. Friday, and the trip there will take approximately six hours. Passengers will have Saturday to shop and browse around Zenith. The train will return to Oakdale on Sunday afternoon.'"

"Cool," John said.

Joe read the next few lines silently. Then he read them aloud: "'All the money made from the trip will go to the Oakdale College Endowment Fund Foundation to support scholarship programs.'"

Wishbone grinned broadly. "Zenith! The big city! I've heard about it, but I've never been there. This is going to be a real adventure! I can hardly wait for the trip to start!" He wagged his tail with joy.

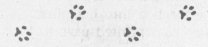

That afternoon, Joe was in his room, deciding what to pack for the trip. Ellen had told him that he would get a costume on the train to wear for the murder-mystery game. However, he still needed some regular clothes for the time he would spend in Zenith.

Joe got his backpack, opened it up, and placed it on his bed. Wishbone leaped up beside it and supervised. Joe packed some jeans, a shirt, and other items. Next, he looked at his bookshelf.

"A murder mystery on a train," Joe said to Wishbone, as he thought about books. "You know, I think there's a mystery novel up in Dad's box of books that has a picture of a train on the cover. Let's go see if we can find it."

Wishbone followed Joe up to the attic, where Joe knelt beside a big box stuffed full of books. He took them out one by one, until he found the book he remembered. It was a paperback, with an old-fashioned steam locomotive on the cover. Joe sat back on his heels and read the title: *Murder on the Orient Express,* by the famous British mystery writer Agatha Christie. He smiled at the book and thought about his dad.

Joe's dad, Steve Talbot, had once been a college basketball coach. He had gotten a rare blood disorder and had died several years before, when Joe was only six. Joe remembered his dad with great affection. One of his best memories was the day that his dad had brought Wishbone home for the first time.

Even after so many years had gone by, Joe was still learning things about who Steve Talbot was. Several months earlier, Joe had found out that his dad had been a big fan of mystery stories. This big box held dozens and dozens of his favorite mystery tales. Some of them were titles that Steve Talbot had read when he himself was a boy.

One by one, Joe was slowly reading these books. He would select one from the box every couple of weeks. He wanted to make them last a long time. Like his father, Joe found that he enjoyed reading mystery stories. It was a lot of fun to try to be smarter and quicker than the detective in figuring out the solution to each case. Joe thought he was getting pretty good at it, too.

"This ought to be a good one," Joe said, reading the back cover of the paperback. "It's a mystery that gets solved by the famous detective Hercule Poirot." Wishbone wagged his tail as if he understood. Joe grinned at him. "Hercule Poirot is a little man with an egg-shaped head. Once he was a detective in Belgium, but now he lives in England. He's a private detective who can unscramble even the most puzzling mysteries. He says he can solve any crime by using his 'little gray cells.' That means his brain," Joe explained to Wishbone.

Joe smiled when he saw Wishbone looking up at him with interest. It was almost as if Wishbone understood him. Joe took the book back downstairs to his room and put it into his backpack.

From downstairs, his mom called, "Are you two ready?"

"Just about," Joe called back.

John said, "I'm packed!"

Joe added, "I don't suppose we need to pack anything other than kibble for Wishbone."

"Just his leash," Ellen called up.

But Wishbone must have had his own idea about that. He raced out of Joe's room. Then he came back carrying something in his mouth. It was one of his favorite squeaky toys, a miniature soccer ball. He jumped up onto the bed and dropped the ball into Joe's backpack.

Joe laughed. "I think he's just packed everything himself," he called out to his mom. Joe rubbed Wishbone's ears. Then he closed all the compartments of his backpack.

Joe and Wishbone went downstairs with the backpack. There Joe found his mom and John, together with Wanda Gilmore. Wanda was a lively woman with very distinct features. She also loved colorful hats. She was wearing a pink hat that went well with her rose-patterned dress. "Hi, Joe," Wanda said cheerfully. "Hello, Wishbone!"

John's blue eyes danced with excitement. "Thanks for inviting me to go along, Miss Gilmore," he said.

"Any friend of Joe's is welcome to come," Wanda told him. "I hope you'll enjoy the play-acting we're all going to do!"

Ellen leaned over to snap Wishbone's leash to his collar. He gave her a sad look. "Don't give me your

15

great big puppy eyes," Ellen said. "I know you don't like your leash, but you have to wear it. Okay, are we all ready?"

"Want me to carry your overnight bag, Mom?" Joe asked.

"Oh, yes, thanks," she said.

Joe picked up Ellen's green-leather bag. "John, will you hold Wishbone's leash?"

"Sure," John said, grinning.

Wanda asked, "Do you have a dog, John?"

John shook his head. "No, but I have two guinea pigs—Chewy and Moomoo."

With a look at Joe, Wanda asked, "Do they dig up flower beds?"

"No," John said, sounding truly surprised at the question.

Joe grinned and said, "Miss Gilmore's teasing you, John. Sometimes Wishbone likes to do a little digging in her yard. It's his one bad habit."

"I *wasn't* teasing," Wanda objected. "I was simply thinking that guinea pigs sound like ideal pets."

Ellen said, "Well, if we're all ready to go—" She fished in her purse and gave Joe her key ring. "Here, Joe. Just put everything in the back of the Explorer."

Joe carried all of the baggage outside to the driveway, where his mom had parked her sport utility vehicle. The back of the Explorer was already half full. Earlier, Wanda had loaded her overnight bag and a couple of hat boxes. They took up a lot of room. Joe unlocked a door and went to work. With some rearranging, Joe got his, John's, and Ellen's luggage packed inside just as the others came out of the Talbots' house.

The group climbed into the vehicle. Ellen backed out of the driveway, and they were off. On the way to the train station, Wanda said, "Joe, you're much too young to remember, of course, but once upon a time eight or ten long-distance passenger trains a day stopped in Oakdale. Now most of the trains passing through are freight trains. I remember my father taking me on just one long train ride when he went to a newspaper convention. I'll bet you've never been on an overnight train trip, have you?"

"No, Miss Gilmore," Joe said, as they drove past Sequoyah Middle School.

"I've been on only one overnight train trip myself," Ellen said. "That was a long time ago. How about you, John?"

"No," John said. "I've never done that. Out in California, everybody uses cars to get around."

Wanda laughed. "Then it will be a whole new experience for you. Oh, this is going to be a lot of fun! Just like something out of an old movie!"

Wishbone, who shared the backseat with Joe and John, stood on his hind legs, looking out a side window. Joe thought he was looking forward to sharing all the fun.

Joe reached over to pet Wishbone. "How about it, buddy?" he asked. "Are you and I going to solve the mystery?"

Wishbone wagged his tail.

"You are going to love the costume ideas I've come up with," Wanda told Joe. "The people in charge of this murder-mystery train trip and I put the passenger list together a month ago. Once that was settled, we rented clothes from antique-clothing and secondhand

17

stores that will make you feel positive you're on an elegant train back in the great days of rail travel in the 1930s. And guess what? We've even set a part aside for Wishbone to play!"

"Hear that, boy?" Joe asked, scratching Wishbone's head. "I hope you can be a good actor. What's the part, Miss Gilmore?"

"Oh, I can't tell you that—yet," answered Wanda, chuckling. "It's going to be a surprise. Ellen, you're going to love your dress!"

"What's it like?" Ellen asked.

"That's a surprise, too!" Wanda said playfully. "We added John to the passenger list when we learned he'd be visiting you. He'll fit right in, though. You'll all find out about your costumes and roles soon enough. Now, the train is going to be eight cars long, not including the locomotive. Behind the steam locomotive is a car called a tender—it carries the coal and water—followed by the baggage car, dining car, three Pullman cars, a buffet-lounge car, and a club car. Ellen, you and I are going to be roommates in one of the Pullman cars."

"Pullman cars?" John asked. "What are those?"

Ellen said, "They're sleeping cars, John. They're actually named after a man, George Pullman. He invented the idea of sleeping cars in the nineteenth century. Each Pullman car is divided into little private rooms, almost like tiny hotel rooms. The rooms are side by side, and each has a door leading out into a narrow corridor that runs the length of the car. In the daytime, you can sit in your compartment and read or play games. Then, at night, the seats fold down into beds you sleep on."

"Right," Wanda said. "Joe, you and Wishbone are

going to share your compartment with John and David. Now, I'm not going to say another word! My lips are sealed! I don't want to spoil any of the fun."

Joe couldn't help laughing. He enjoyed Wanda's sense of enthusiasm. She loved to cook up surprises, and she enjoyed doing anything out of the ordinary.

Ellen steered the Ford Explorer into the parking lot at the Oakdale train station. There stood a red-brick building with a green-tile roof. Ellen pulled into a parking spot, and then everyone got out of the vehicle.

Joe had just borrowed his mom's key to unlock the rear door of the Explorer when he heard a cheery voice say, "Hi!"

He turned in surprise. Samantha Kepler—"Sam" to her friends—and David Barnes were grinning at him. "Hi!" Joe said. "Are you two ready for this neat trip?"

Sam said, "I am, but I think my dad is even more excited. He loves old trains," she explained, as she helped Joe unload the baggage. "He jumped at the chance to go on the trip."

"I wish that my parents and Emily could have come along, too, but my sister has a dance recital tomorrow," David said, taking some of Wanda's gear out of the Explorer.

"This is going to be great," Joe said. "Wishbone's coming along for the ride, so we're all together. Oh, let me introduce you to someone. This is John Hancock. He's visiting us from California!"

"Hi, John," Sam said. "My name's Samantha Kepler, but all my good friends call me Sam."

"Mine's David Barnes," David told him. "And everyone calls me David."

"Hi," John said, grinning. "Joe's already told me a lot about you."

Joe clapped John on the shoulder. "We'll make John a part of our team," he said. "We'll solve this mystery together."

"We don't even know what the mystery is yet," David pointed out. "But you're right. The four of us will make a perfect mystery-solving team."

Wishbone headed toward Sam, pulling hard at his leash. He tugged John along. Sam laughed and bent over to give the dog's ears an especially good rubbing. "I think Wishbone's trying to tell us something," she said. "He's saying that the *five* of us will make a perfect mystery-solving team!"

"That's right," Joe said, slamming the Explorer's rear door closed. "With the four of us along, and Wishbone to help, the other detectives just won't stand a chance!"

Wishbone barked as if he completely agreed.

Chapter Two

*H*onk! The deep blare of a car horn made Joe turn around. He looked and laughed. "Oh, it's Mr. Zimmerman!" he said, pointing at a beautiful antique car just rolling into the parking lot.

The old Hudson came to a stop, and a strongly built, smiling man climbed out. "Hi, kids!" he called in a deep voice. "Hello, Ellen. Hi, Wanda."

Horace Zimmerman was a good friend of Wanda's. He was also a successful businessman and collected classic cars. Joe, Sam, and David had first met Mr. Zimmerman when he had helped save and restore the Moonlight Drive-In Theater just outside of town.

"Hi, Mr. Zimmerman," Joe said. "Are you going on this trip, too?"

"Wouldn't miss it!" Horace answered, smiling widely. "I love old cars, but close behind them, I love old trains! I hope Wishbone's ready for an adventure, too!"

"I think he is," Sam said, grinning. "He *looks* ready, anyway," she said, as she watched Wishbone strain at his leash.

"Wonderful!" Horace chuckled.

Joe introduced John to Mr. Zimmerman, and Horace shook hands. Then he said in a pleased tone of voice, "Delighted to meet you!" He opened the trunk of his Hudson and took out an elegant-looking black-leather suitcase. "Well, come on! Let's go out and see this wonderful train."

The group walked across the parking lot and into the train station. Joe liked the station a lot. It was usually a quiet place, and very old-fashioned. Long wooden benches with swirling wrought-iron armrests took up most of the waiting room. At one end of the room was a ticket window, although it was closed. The walls were decorated with plaster cupids' heads, and sculpted clusters of grapes were high up near the ceiling. Some of them were cracked.

"It's a shame that this historic train station has become so rundown," Wanda said with a sigh. "I'll have to get the Oakdale Historical Society to work on preserving what was once a lovely train station."

Joe smiled at her enthusiasm. He admired all of Wanda's good work in the community. Wanda owned the Oakdale newspaper, the *Chronicle,* and she was also the president of the Oakdale Historical Society. Wanda loved history. Thanks to her, many of Oakdale's older buildings had been saved and preserved.

Wanda had bought the old Oakdale fire station years before, when it was about to be torn down. She had raised money to fix it up. Now Travis Del Rio was renting the space from her. His sporting-goods business, located in the old fire station, had some unique features no other store like it had—including a fire pole in the middle of the floor space.

"Come on, my friends," Horace said, opening a wide wooden door. "Here's the platform, and here— Oh, my goodness! What a wonderful old train!"

"Would you take a look at that!" exclaimed Wanda.

Joe whistled. He had seen the picture on the flyer, but the sight of the real *Zenith Condor* filled him with a sense of amazement. "It's really great!" he said. "I've never seen any train like it."

The train waited at the edge of the platform. The eight main cars were all a gleaming pewter-silver metal. Dark blue window frames trimmed in yellow ran along the sides. Aluminum stripes ran along the edges of the roof line of all the cars. Off to Joe's right, the huge locomotive sat, its engine already humming, waiting to pull its attached cars.

"You won't see many trains like this one," Horace told Joe. "Not these days. This is a real classic. The locomotive is a Hudson-type streamlined steam engine. It has four pilot wheels, two on each side—those are the small wheels up front. Then on each side there are three driving wheels, the huge ones that provide the power. And, finally, on each side there are two trailing wheels, the smaller ones under the cab. The cab is where the engineer works and where the operating controls are."

"It's almost like a sculpture," Ellen said. "I thought all steam locomotives were big and black."

"Oh, no," Horace told her. "Have you ever heard of Henry Dreyfus?"

Everyone in the group shook their heads no.

Horace grinned. "Well, it so happens that Henry Dreyfus was a train designer earlier in this century. He

designed the *Zenith Condor,* and he also designed other famous trains, like the *Twentieth-Century Limited.* Mr. Dreyfus was a real artist. He liked the curved lines and gracefulness you see in the *Condor.* He also designed it to be a very fast train."

"It looks really powerful," John said.

"It is," Horace replied. "Now, look way down at the very back end of the train."

Joe looked back along the train. "That's not a caboose," he said.

Horace laughed. "No, it certainly is not. Saying that's a caboose is like saying a giant California red-wood tree is only a weed! It's a private club car. The *Condor* used to be one of the main trains owned by the Windom Railroad Company. Once upon a time, that club car was the car that the wealthy Windom family reserved for its own use. It even has a name— the Windom Traveler. Many years ago, when rail travel was popular, quite a few rich families had their own private railway cars built. They were like elegant, box-sized homes on wheels. The families paid rail-road companies to attach their private cars to the back of regular trains. That way, they could travel separately from regular folks, and in luxury and splendor."

"The car looks almost new," Wanda said.

"That's because it has been in a museum for years," Horace explained. "It was originally built in France, way back in 1939. It was shipped to the United States for use by the Windom family the week before France was invaded by Germany at the very beginning of World War Two. There's even a spy story connected to the car."

That interested Joe. "What kind of a spy story?" he asked.

"Well," Horace said, "the Windoms helped a lot of people who had to escape from Nazi Germany before and during World War Two. Supposedly, they allowed the people who were fleeing from the Nazi government to ship valuables to the United States. They did that by having the builders create special hiding places on this car and many of their railcars. The Traveler was the last car to be shipped out of Europe before the war broke out. The story says the car carried millions of dollars' worth of hidden treasure. Unfortunately, some of it was lost—and it's never been found!"

Joe felt a growing sense of excitement. "Then it could still be in there!"

Shaking his head, Horace said, "I'm afraid not. The car was used from 1939 up until about 1964 by the Windom Railroad Company. Then it was taken out of service and sent to the Windom Railroad Museum in Zenith. It was completely taken apart and restored. No, anything that might once have been hidden in there must be long gone. Still, the car has a very exciting history."

A sudden, loud *chuff!* of escaping steam made Joe jump. Wishbone barked. Another white cloud of steam escaped from it as it waited to begin its run.

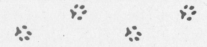

The sound of hissing steam startled Wishbone. It was a noise he rarely heard, and he sniffed deeply. "Let's see—smells like water! In fact, it smells like

26

steam, the kind that comes out of the kettle when Ellen boils water for tea. But it sounds like a huge sniffing dog—a dog about the size of a gymnasium! And look at all the people!"

More people had been making their way out onto the platform while Horace, Ellen, Wanda, and the kids looked at the train. Many others were there. All of them held hand luggage and talked excitedly. Wishbone tugged at his leash impatiently, but John kept a tight grip on it.

John asked, "Joe, is it okay if I take Wishbone exploring a little?"

Joe looked at Ellen. He said, "Mom?"

Ellen looked down at Wishbone, who gave her his I'll-be-on-my-best-behavior look. "Well," Ellen said slowly, "I suppose he won't get you into any trouble. John, keep a good grip on his leash, though."

"Okay. Go ahead, boy," John said.

Wishbone trotted off at once. "Thanks! We'll take a quick sniff around. Then we'll get back to the rest of you! Oh, wow! I hope some of these people brought snacks!"

A man in a dark blue uniform had pushed a big-wheeled cart out onto the platform. He was starting to put baggage tags on all the luggage and stack them on the cart. Wishbone watched him for a minute. Then he heard a familiar rumbly voice come from behind him.

"I tell you, Quentin, it's the lead car!"

Wishbone whirled around. Mr. Kilgore Gurney, the stout, bearded, cheerful owner of Rendezvous Books, stood nearby. Wishbone wagged his tail excitedly upon seeing the familiar figure.

The previous summer, Joe had worked in the

bookstore for Mr. Gurney. He and his old friend, Dr. Quentin Quarrel, were partners in the bookstore now. Both of them liked to give snacks to friendly, handsome dogs. At least, they had usually come through for Wishbone.

Mr. Gurney was squinting at a ticket. Behind him was the tall, thin Dr. Quarrel, a retired college professor. Wishbone tugged John toward them.

Dr. Quarrel took out his own ticket. "Now, look," he said. "Kilgore, if you will take the time to read your ticket, you'll see it's for car three. How could car three be the lead car?"

Wishbone greeted the two men with a friendly bark. They both smiled back and leaned over to pet him. John introduced himself. Then the excited Wishbone pulled John away. He trotted down the platform, sniffing other friends.

He saw Dr. Maddy Kingston, a computer expert at the Oakdale College Natural History Museum. She had black hair and wore glasses. The museum had *big* bones—dinosaur bones! The dog remembered when a dinosaur exhibit had arrived at the museum, and David helped with the computer system there. Wishbone loved the exhibit, because he loved bones!

Just past her, Walter Kepler, Sam's dad, stood talking to the man in the dark blue uniform. Wishbone took an especially deep sniff. Mmm! Walter Kepler owned and operated Pepper Pete's Pizza Parlor, and he usually smelled a little like pepperoni, hamburger, and sausage—at least to Wishbone!

"Why, hi, there, Wishbone!"

Wishbone spun around, grinning at the sound of the familiar new voice. Just coming onto the platform, his overnight bag and ticket in his hand, was Travis Del Rio. The owner of Oakdale Sports & Games was a good friend of both Joe and Wishbone. The dog trotted over to Travis, who gave him a good pat. "Hi, Travis! Great to see you! Uh . . . this is our house guest, John Hancock!"

"Hi," John said. "I'm John Hancock. I'm staying with the Talbots for a few days."

"That sounds great. I hope you're enjoying your time in Oakdale. Well, where are Ellen and Joe?" Travis asked, looking around.

"Last time I saw them they were by the locomotive," said John.

Wishbone's nose twitched. "Right this way! Follow me! The noble dog will lead you!" Wishbone ran along the platform, and Travis followed.

Ellen looked around as Wishbone came up. "Hello, Travis!" she said, sounding delighted. "I'm glad you decided to come."

Travis laughed. "I made up my mind at the last moment. The kids are visiting their aunt, and with spring break the town's going to be empty this weekend, so I thought, *why not?* So here I am. I understand I bought the very last ticket."

Wishbone's tail thumped against the train station platform. "This is gonna be so much fun! It's like a vacation, except we're taking almost the whole town along! I just hope that railroad food is tasty— *Yikes!* What's that?"

A loud whistle pierced the air. Joe looked back toward the station door, wondering what the shrill noise was. He saw a man in a dark blue railway conductor's uniform. He held a silver whistle to his lips and blew it again, immediately getting everyone's attention.

"Welcome, everyone!" the conductor shouted. "Now, before we board, I'd like you to listen to just a few words from the people who are in charge of this special train trip. If you will all come to the far end of the platform, we'll get started!"

Everyone crowded toward the back of the platform. Joe looked at a stage that had been specially built for the occasion near the end of the train station. Red, white, and blue ribbons were draped across the stage. Near the front was a lectern with a microphone attached to it. At the microphone was a woman Joe recognized.

It was Margaret Bradbury, the chief executive officer of the Windom Foundation. Behind her was Mr. Bob Pruitt. He had been Joe, Sam, and David's English teacher two years before. He was a quiet, scholarly looking man. Also behind Ms. Bradbury was the conductor.

Joe did not know the other two people on the stage. They were a man and a woman who looked like brother and sister. Both were tall, blond, and slim. They wore identical outfits: gray slacks and blue sweaters.

Ms. Bradbury said grandly, "Thank you all so much for coming on our special trip. You are helping greatly to support the Oakdale College Endowment Fund Foundation. I know you are going to have a good time. I'd like to introduce our volunteer conductors. Our first conductor is Mr. Henry Cooper. Henry, blow your whistle again!"

With a grin, the man in the conductor's outfit blew a high note. Wishbone squirmed so much that Joe took his leash from John. Joe picked Wishbone up, thinking that his dog might like to see what was going on. "Hey, stay still," he said to the wiggling Jack Russell terrier.

Ms. Bradbury continued. "Mr. Cooper works for the Windom Railroad Museum in Zenith. He's going to look after this beautiful train for us!"

Everyone applauded.

Next, Ms. Bradbury introduced Mr. Pruitt. "Our second conductor is Bob Pruitt. He also has a special part to play in this adventure," she said. "You'll see what I mean later. Anyway, if you need anything, please just ask me, Mr. Cooper, or Mr. Pruitt," said Ms. Bradbury.

Finally, Ms. Bradbury turned and motioned for

the blond man and woman to step forward to the microphone.

"Come on over," she said. "Ladies and gentlemen, let me introduce to you Monica and Michael Patterson. They are the owners of Mystery Murders, Incorporated! I'm going to let them tell you about the game we will soon begin to play."

The two stepped over to the microphone. With a smile, Michael Patterson said, "Thank you! Now, then, I hope everyone is ready to become an actor! Once you are aboard this train, forget your ordinary, day-to-day life. You will become a new person. My sister, Monica, and I will hand out envelopes to everyone—right before you board."

Monica then spoke. "You will find details in the envelope on the character you are to play. A little later, you will get your costumes. I'd just like to take a moment to thank Wanda Gilmore and Ellen Talbot for helping us do research on the outfits you'll wear. Now, please join in the spirit of the game! Become your character! And pay close attention to everything that happens— there just may be a murder to solve!"

The Pattersons stepped back, and Ms. Bradbury nodded to Mr. Cooper. He blew his whistle again and shouted, "All-ll aboard! All aboard! The *Zenith Condor* is ready to board! Hurry, folks! We will leave at five o'clock sharp!"

"This is going to be so cool!" John said from beside Joe. "Come on!"

After Joe put Wishbone down, he moved along with the crowd. Joe felt eager and excited to board the train. This was a whole new experience, and he was enjoying every minute of it!

Wishbone's Well-Trained Dictionary

Hello, gang! Wishbone here! Does all our train talk have you sidetracked? Have no fear! Just chug on into our well-trained dictionary, and you'll be on the right track in no time!

berth   a sleeping place or bunk in a Pullman car

buffet-lounge   a railway car where cold snacks and drinks are served

club car   a railroad car with lounge chairs and, usually, a refreshment bar

compartment   a small private room in a sleeping car

conductor   the official in charge of the passengers. He also collects the fares and tickets.

engineer   the driver of a railroad locomotive

express   a train that makes very few stops. It travels faster than a local train.

local	a train that stops at every train station. It is a slower train than an express.
locomotive	the engine of the train
porter	a railroad employee who waits on the passengers in a dining car or Pullman sleeper
Pullman car	a railroad car with private compartments or seats that can be made up into beds for sleeping
roundhouse	a circular or semicircular building with a turntable in the center. It is used for storing, repairing, and switching locomotives.
siding	a short track to one side of the main railroad that is joined to it at one or both ends by a switch
switch	a section of railroad track that can rotate in one direction or another
tender	small car, attached to the end of a locomotive, that holds water and coal
yard engine	a locomotive that moves railway cars short distances
yard master	the man in charge of all trains in the station

Chapter Three

Carrying his backpack and holding Wishbone's leash, Joe followed his mother up the portable wooden box-style steps and onto the train. They got on a car named the City of Miami. As Joe tried to keep his backpack from bumping against the wall, they walked down a carpeted aisle. It was so narrow that Joe could easily have touched both walls at once. The walls were made of highly polished panels of dark wood. Each compartment had a bright silvery door set into it. Overhead, light fixtures made the dark brown wood gleam and the dark blue carpet look rich and thick, like velvet. Wishbone trotted noiselessly between Ellen and Joe.

"Three, four, five . . ." Ellen counted the doors as she went. "Six . . . seven . . . Oh, here we are—compartment number eight. This is the room I'll share with Wanda." Ellen stopped in front of an elegant silver door. Framing the door were bands of dark blue aluminum, similar to what was on the outside of the train. A small silver "8" was in the center of one blue band. Ellen unlocked the door and stepped inside.

From the doorway, Joe looked in. The room was quite small, about eight feet square. "Will there be enough room for two people?" he asked.

"Of course. It's just lovely!" Ellen said.

Ellen picked up her overnight bag. They stepped inside and looked around. The compartment had two curtained windows. Under the windows was a dark blue sofa with yellow stripes and silver trim. Opposite the sofa, on each side of the door, were two low-backed, bucket-style easy chairs. A little round table stood between the left wall and the sofa. Wishbone sniffed around.

Joe asked, "Mom, don't you get a bed?"

With a laugh, Ellen said, "Wanda and I get two beds. That's why the compartment is called a double. You'll have a compartment like this one to share with David and John, except yours will be a triple."

Joe glanced around the neat little room again. "Mom, I don't see any beds."

Ellen smiled. "You will in just a moment," she said. She pressed a button by the door. A panel on the side wall gently slid out and down. The panel supported a neatly made-up, narrow bed with a blanket in the *Zenith Condor* colors. "The sofa turns into a bed, too. Many years ago, in the golden age of train travel, a porter would do this."

"A porter?" Joe asked.

"Yes," his mother said. "Porters were railway workers whose job it was to take care of passengers. They did everything from cleaning clothes to making up beds to delivering room-service meals. Times change—now we have to take care of all the details ourselves."

Joe was inspecting the fold-out bunk. He admired the way it took up so little space. "That's tricky!" he said with a laugh.

"And it's in the way," his mother replied, swinging the panel back into place. "If you want to look around the compartment, go ahead. I need to unpack. Then you ought to go find David and John. You're in the next car back, I think. Here's your ticket." Joe took the ticket from her.

While Ellen unpacked, Joe explored. A narrow door near one end of the sofa opened into a small bathroom. At the other end of the sofa, drawers slid out of the walls. More drawers were under the sofa. Joe was impressed by how the small compartment had so much storage space. Wishbone made himself at home in one of the rounded easy chairs. From there he watched Joe and Ellen.

"Here are the costumes!" Ellen said. She had opened a narrow closet hidden in a corner next to the sofa. Inside the closet were garment bags. "Let me see. . . . This one is labeled 'Gilmore,' and the other one is mine."

Joe watched as his mom finished unzipping the bag. She looked startled.

"What's wrong?" he asked.

"There's been a mistake," Ellen said, grinning. "This one's labeled 'Talbot,' but I suspect it's yours, not mine!" She zipped up the bag and handed it to Joe.

Excited, Joe quickly unzipped the bag and looked at the clothes inside. On a wooden hanger were an old-fashioned pair of short, baggy brown pants. Joe also found a crisp white shirt with a red bowtie. Pinned to the shirt were long black socks and a large, soft gray cap. In one plastic bag was an old notebook with a bulky fountain pen clipped to the cover. In another plastic bag were a pair of black shoes. "Great, Mom!" he said. He took the costume out of the bag to get a better look at it. "But what am I supposed to be?"

Ellen looked back inside the closet. "Ah, here's mine!" she said, pulling out another garment bag. She unzipped it and took out a long gray chiffon dress. "Oh, this is beautiful!"

"What am I supposed to be?" Joe asked again.

Ellen turned to him with a smile. "I wish I could tell you, Joe, but I just don't know. I worked with Wanda to do research on the costumes. But then she and the Pattersons created the characters."

Joe put his costume back into the garment bag. "But if we don't know who we are, how can we solve the murder?"

"Oh, we'll find out who we are soon enough." Ellen carefully took the dress out of the garment bag and off its hanger. She laid it down on the sofa and opened her purse. She pulled out three manila envelopes. She handed two to Joe. One envelope was addressed to him, and the other to Wishbone. Across the top of each envelope, someone had written in large red block letters, DO NOT OPEN! A typewritten note had been stapled to each envelope.

Joe read his:

> You are invited to a murder!
> This envelope contains all you need to know to play our exciting game of mystery! Are you a suspect, a detective, a victim, or even the murderer? Just

bring this envelope with you to the
buffet-lounge car at 6:00 P.M., and all
will be explained! Then you're on your
own!

Have a Happy Mystery!

Monica and Michael Patterson,
Mystery Murders, Incorporated

"Well," Joe said, staring at his envelope, "it looks
like the first mystery is what's in these!"

His mother laughed. "And the only way to solve it
is to get dressed and join everyone else in the buffet-
lounge. Do you want to find your berth first, or do you
want to get dressed here?"

"My berth?" Joe asked.

"That means your sleeping compartment," Ellen
explained.

"Oh." Joe made up his mind. "I'll go there and
change. I want to see what it looks like, anyway. Maybe
John and David are already there."

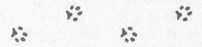

"Whoa! Neat smells, new smells, fancy smells!
What an adventure, huh, Joe?" An excited Wishbone
trotted next to Joe and fought the urge to run ahead.
The train started, and Wishbone braced his legs.
"Whoops! The floor is moving—is it supposed to do
that?" Wishbone followed Joe into the buffet-lounge
of the *Zenith Condor*.

The buffet-lounge car was the next-to-last car on

the train. In it, at the far end, Wishbone saw a long bar with high, round-seated stools in front of it. On the other side of the car, tables and chairs were spaced out next to the windows. There was also a small white piano at the end of the car.

Wishbone blinked. Familiar people filled the car. All of them wore interesting, old-fashioned costumes. They laughed and admired one another. A boy in a long white lab coat and large round glasses waved as he made his way through the crowd toward them.

Wishbone wagged his tail. "David. Let's see . . . what character could you be playing?"

"Hi, Joe!" David said with a grin. "I expected to see you in our compartment. What sort of pants are those? Are you sure you're supposed to wear them like that?"

Joe tugged at his pants. The short legs came down only to his knees. "They're called plus-fours. You wear the socks up to your knees and fasten the pants legs on top of them. Do they look funny?"

David shrugged. "I suppose they're the 1930s version of shorts."

A light flashed, startling Wishbone. He whirled, then relaxed. A smiling John Hancock was just lowering an old-fashioned camera from his eyes. "Gotcha!" he said, stepping forward. He was wearing a kind of raincoat called a trenchcoat. It looked like a military-style coat, and was dark green. He also wore a battered brown hat with a card in the band that said PRESS in big red letters. "I'm guessing, based on my costume, that I play a newspaper photographer," he said.

"Good guess. We'll find out soon who we'll be playing," Joe said.

Wishbone was getting used to the rumbling

movement of the train. "And I'm hungry! Excuse me—I'm going to see if anyone has a snack for the dog!"

As Wishbone trotted away, David nudged Joe. "Want to see a really great costume? Just take a look at Sam. She's over there," David said, pointing.

Joe looked over just as Sam stepped out of the crowd. His eyes grew wide. Sam was usually a jeans-and-T-shirt person. But now she looked very different.

Sam wore a long white dress of silk and lace, and gloves. Her blond hair was held back in a wreath of white-silk roses. She turned red when she saw the look on Joe's face. "I feel silly," she said.

Joe shook his head. "Oh, no, Sam. It's really kind of neat."

"Well," she said, "this is not me."

David grinned. "Be an actor! Play the part!"

John's camera looked old-fashioned, but it took instant pictures. He held up the one that had just developed. "David's right," he said. "Look at this shot of David and Joe. Don't they look like actors?"

"Once I find out what character I'm going to be, I'll try to play my part," Sam said. "Anyway, you should see my dad. He *really* looks different."

"I think I look dashing," Walter Kepler said with dignity as he joined the group.

Sam smiled at her father. He wore a tan British army officer's uniform, complete with a sun helmet and a chest full of medals. "I think you look great, Dad."

"Thanks, Sam," he said, giving her a hug.

"Well, since everyone's in costume, at least I don't stand out," Sam said.

Before Joe could speak, someone banged a wooden gavel on a table to get everyone's attention. "May I have your attention, please?" called a loud, clear voice. Everyone turned. Mr. Pruitt stood behind a table. He was wearing an elegant white dinner jacket and dark trousers. He banged on the table once again, until the crowd grew silent. "On behalf of the Windom Railroad Company, the Oakdale College Endowment Fund Foundation, and Mystery Murders, Incorporated, I want to welcome you all aboard for the Great *Zenith Condor* Murder Game!"

A cheer went up from the crowd. Mr. Pruitt waved a brown envelope. "Has everybody brought their envelopes?" Everyone in the car raised their envelopes high in the air. "Great!" Mr. Pruitt looked at his watch. "Then open them all . . . wait for it . . . wait for it . . . right now!"

Joe had been carrying his envelope under his arm. He ripped it open and took out three typewritten pages. He also found a name tag and read it aloud: "Michael O'Hara."

"All right," Mr. Pruitt called in the same voice he used to get his students' attention: "The pages in your envelopes describe the character you are going to play for the next two days! Read them carefully. As soon as you have, you will no longer be you! Dig deeply into your imagination. You will all become passengers on the great *Zenith Condor,* roaring toward Zenith on a day back in 1938! War is about to break out in Europe, Asia, and the South Pacific. Spies, thugs, and gangsters are lurking everywhere!

"Everything you need to know is in your information packets! Most of it you can share with other people. But watch out for the parts that are underlined in red! You can give that information to people only if they specifically ask for it. Oh, and if there's anything underlined in green, keep that *very* secret! No one must know that information. It means you're the murderer! Well, good hunting, everyone!"

Joe, John, Sam, and David joined in the crowd's cheers. Then they went off to read their instructions. Sam said she was staying in the buffet-lounge.

Wishbone, David, John, and Joe walked back to their compartment. It was a little like his mom's and Wanda's, except it had two swing-down berths, as well as the sofa that folded out into a bed.

Joe sat on the sofa and read his pages carefully. David and John each sat in one of the easy chairs. They studied their descriptions, too.

"I'm Elvin Morse," John announced. "I'm a newspaper photographer assigned to cover the trip. And I'm supposed to be working with you, Joe."

Wishbone jumped up on the sofa and craned his neck. It seemed as if he was trying to get a peek at Joe's papers.

"Watch out, Joe," David warned. "I think Wishbone's trying to read your character sheets."

Joe laughed. "Wishbone's pretty smart, but he's not *that* smart!"

"Neat," David said, finishing his reading and folding his own sheets. "Get this, guys—my name's John Kindler. I'm a brilliant young scientist at Oakdale College. Now I'm on my way to Zenith to join other top scientists working on military-defense projects.

This is too cool! But I don't have any red underlining on my sheets."

"Ah, but the really important question is, do you have any *green* underlining?" Joe said. He stared suspiciously at his friend. He opened his notebook and held his pen over it. "Tell me the truth!"

"That, sir, is a very personal question," David replied with a grin.

"I'm *supposed* to ask nosy questions," Joe said. He held out his hand. "Allow me to introduce myself. My name is Michael O'Hara. I'm a cub reporter—that means I don't have a whole lot of experience yet. I am working for *The Oakdale Chronicle*. My paper received an anonymous tip that something exciting might happen on this train. Getting a scoop—being the first to report an important story—could give me my big break and make me a famous journalist. So I'm traveling with Elvin Morse, here, to write the big story. I have to find out as much as I can about everyone. And I'm not going to tell you if I have any red underlining."

David laughed and said, "Come on. Let's go find Sam and see what role she's playing."

They went back to the buffet-lounge, and John said, "There she is!"

Sam stood near one of the picture windows, just putting her character sheets back in the envelope. Joe led the way over to her. "Well," he said, "who are you?"

Mr. Kepler tapped Joe on the shoulder. "Excuse me, young man, but the young lady should not be speaking to you," he said, trying for a British accent.

"She shouldn't?" David said.

"Uh . . . why not, sir?" Joe asked.

"Because you have not been properly introduced.

44

A proper young lady does not speak with those to whom she has not been correctly introduced."

"A lady?" John asked, sounding surprised.

"Quite right," said Mr. Kepler. He saluted, then turned away.

For a moment, the guys all stood looking at one another. "How do we handle this?" Joe wondered. "We can't talk to her until we're properly introduced."

"And there's no one to introduce us," David said. "That's a problem!"

Sam turned red.

John cleared his throat, looking at Sam's name tag. "I beg your pardon . . . uh . . . Lady Kincade. I believe we met in . . . uh . . . New York City, not very long ago. I photographed you as you arrived from Southampton on that great ocean liner. It was called . . . uh . . . the *Queen of the Seas*."

"Good thinking, Elvin!" Joe whispered, relieved.

Sam extended her gloved hand. "Yes, I do recall making your acquaintance. I am Lady Victoria Kincade. I live in London. My family owns farmland in East Africa—near Mombasa and Durban, along the coast. We also own vast amounts of land in the dry interior regions. I am the sole heiress to the fabulous Kincade Diamond Mines! You may present your friends."

John quickly introduced Joe as Michael O'Hara, and David as John Kindler.

"You must be very wealthy," David said. "Maybe you'd like to invest in some important scientific experiments that will have worldwide effects!"

"Fabulous diamond mines?" asked Joe.

"Unbelievably fabulous. At least"—Sam held up the envelope—"that's what it says here. I hope I can do this right. Will you guys help me?"

"Well," Joe said, "just remember, I'm Michael O'Hara, reporter. If I can find out how to play *that* part, then I'll try to help you!"

David laughed. "I'm glad my folks didn't make me stay for Emily's recital. This mystery trip is going to be tons of fun!"

Sam began, "Joe . . ."

"Michael O'Hara, cub reporter. And I hope I'll soon be an ace reporter." Joe couldn't help grinning. The experience so far was a lot like being in a play—except that he made up the lines as he went along, instead of reading from a prepared script.

"Fine—Michael O'Hara, then. You haven't opened up Wishbone's envelope. What did the Pattersons come up with for him?"

"Yeah," David said. "What kind of a part can a dog have?"

"Well, there's only one way to find out!" Joe ripped open the manila envelope with Wishbone's name on it. He pulled out the character description, then read it with deep concentration.

After a while, Sam asked Joe, "Well . . . Mr. O'Hara . . . what does it say?"

Joe looked up with a grin. "Well, on this trip, Wishbone is a pedigreed Russian wolfhound! He's big, strong, and handsome. His name is Borshoi."

"Borshoi!" John repeated with a laugh.

"He has a weakness for French Champagne and steak-and-kidney-pies! At least he doesn't have any green underlining." Joe grinned.

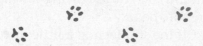

"Great! A custom-made role! I might need a touch of makeup, though!" Wishbone stood at attention. "Borshoi the wolfhound, reporting for duty. How about a snack? You can hold the Champagne, but bring on that steak-and-kidney-pie!"

Chapter Four

Joe, David, John, and Wishbone returned to their compartment. They decided who would sleep where—John and Joe got the swing-down bunks, and David got the sofa bed.

Then, with Joe still feeling a little uncertain about being Michael O'Hara, the boys reviewed the directions on their character sheets. It was nearly seven o'clock, and the whole group was supposed to gather in the buffet-lounge car at seven.

A party was going on when they got there. Lights came on as the sun went down. Joe was amazed at how real everything seemed. Someone was playing "Stardust," a tune from the 1930s, on the piano. The women wore beautiful long gowns and sparkling bracelets and necklaces, while the men were dressed in old-fashioned military uniforms or suits with wide lapels and baggy trousers. It was as if the present had disappeared and 1938 had taken its place. Outside the train's wide windows, shadowy hills and trees whizzed by. Now and then the locomotive gave long blasts of its whistle. The floor underfoot rattled and vibrated as the train clickety-clacked along the track bed.

David brought Joe a glass of pink-grapefruit punch. "Great make-up and costumes," David said as he looked around. "Just look at your mom!"

Joe nodded, a big smile on his face. His mom was wearing her long, elegant, gray dress. She chatted pleasantly with Michael and Monica Patterson. She held a Champagne glass filled with sparkling white grape juice. The twins wore stylish white tennis clothes of the 1930s.

Joe heard his mom say, "Of course—my publisher was upset! But I told him that great literature just can't be rushed. He should be thrilled that I'm writing a book for him at all!" She laughed, obviously having a great time.

Ellen had told Joe that she was Marjory MacBride, a best-selling novelist with a mysterious past. She had refused to tell him *why* her past was mysterious. Joe decided that one of his jobs as a reporter would be to find out!

"Excuse me, excuse me! Coming through!" The boys and Wishbone were eased out of the way by Wanda Gilmore. She came sailing down the aisle in the largest hat Joe had ever seen. There were so many artificial flowers stacked on it that she looked like a vase stuffed full of roses.

"Excuse me, Miss Gil——" Joe started to say.

Wanda placed one finger on her lips, then pointed at her name tag with the other. "Why, Mr. O'Hara, don't you recognize me?"

Joe read the name tag. "Oh . . . uh . . . sorry, Miss . . . uh . . . Nordecker?"

Wanda tapped him on the shoulder. "Do *not* play the young innocent with me, Michael O'Hara! You, Mr. Morse, there, and I all work for the same newspaper! You know perfectly well that I am the paper's famous gossip columnist, Noreen 'Nosy' Nordecker. I am hot on the trail of my latest major story. If you want to beat me to the punch, you'll have to work hard!" She turned around dramatically. Then she winked at Joe and whispered, "I have to turn sideways to get between cars. I love hats, but this one is just too much!" She continued on her way.

Mr. Kilgore Gurney and Dr. Quentin Quarrel had already found places to sit at one of the tables. They might be playing characters in the murder-mystery game, but they had their own favorite other game, too. They were playing their version of chess. They made up and changed the rules as they went along.

Mr. Gurney was dressed in a black suit with a string tie. His name tag said he was "Dr. Mortimer

Stitcher." He was staring at the board with a look of disappointment on his face.

He muttered, "I still say they made a mistake. This is *your* character, Quentin. He's even got your suit."

Dr. Quarrel smiled at his business partner. Dr. Quarrel wore a khaki suit. His white pith helmet—Joe thought of it as a jungle explorer's hat—lay on the table next to him. "I am a perfect choice for 'Professor Zebulon Dire,'" he said. "I am a well-known archeologist. In fact, I'm the leading expert on Africa's Great Zimbabwe Ruins—you know, the massive stone-walled fortress that was built perhaps thousands of years ago by an extremely advanced culture that then seemed to have vanished. After all, Kilgore, I *do* have a real-life Ph.D. Check."

"You're a doctor of *philosophy*, Quentin!" grumbled Mr. Gurney. "You don't know the first thing about— Wait! Check? Where? Hey! There are *three* black bishops on this board!"

Dr. Quarrel looked innocent. "Well, of course. We're playing according to the Constantinople rules, aren't we?"

Mr. Gurney glared at him. "There's no such thing as the Constantinople rules! You're cheating again, Quentin!"

Dr. Quarrel smiled. "And I'm doing it very well, I might add. It took you half an hour to notice! Double-check."

"There's no such thing as double-check!" Mr. Gurney roared.

Joe, John, and David slipped by the men, shaking their heads as they went. The two old friends couldn't play a regular game of chess if their lives depended on it. But Joe had learned that both of them enjoyed their unusual approach to the game. And they liked to argue. In fact, Joe thought, if Mr. Gurney and Dr. Quarrel ever began to be polite to each other, that would mean they were angry with each other!

Joe saw Sam at the front of the buffet-lounge car. "Good evening, Lady Veronica!" Joe called, as he and his friends came up to Sam. Wishbone walked over to Sam, and she began to feed him cocktail sausages from a silver tray.

Sam tried to seem snobbish, but she couldn't help giggling. Then she tried her play-acting routine again. "That's Lady *Victoria,* sir. And I am looking after this handsome Russian wolfhound that was so cruelly abandoned by his original owner."

"Don't let him give you his 'starving dog' act, Your Ladyship," Joe said. "I know this dog. He has plenty of his favorite kibble back in his compartment." He lowered his voice and whispered, "Are you having as much fun as we are?"

"Yes . . . lots—but not as much as Dad!" Sam stopped and corrected herself. "That is, not as much as my guardian, Colonel Richard Aberdeen. He's having a blast! He's even starting to talk with a proper English accent." She sighed. "This is so hard. I only hope I'm acting my part right."

Joe chuckled. "Can you walk with us? I know as a lady you have strict behavior rules. You can even bring the wolfhound if you want to."

Sam took a slim book from a purse she had with her. She pretended to look something up in it. "There doesn't seem to be anything in the *Rules for Ladies* about walking. I suppose it would be all right," she said, putting the book away.

"You have a rule book?" David asked suspiciously. "Hey, no fair! I didn't get a rule book. Did you get a rule book, Joe?"

Joe shrugged. "Nope. I guess it takes more studying to be a lady of royal blood than it does to be a scientist or a reporter."

"And Borshoi will come with us," Sam said, patting Wishbone on the head.

Wishbone walked through a forest of adult legs. He kept pace with Joe and his friends. *This costume party is fun! With makeup and costumes, few of these people look familiar, but my nose tells me I know every one of them! Disguises! Mystery! I love it! Beware, suspects! "The nose" knows!*

The kids walked toward the back of the buffet-lounge car.

David stopped and pointed. Joe and Sam followed his direction. Wishbone felt his ears perk up. "Whoa! A woman sitting *on* a piano! And I get in trouble for jumping up onto the table!"

Maddy Kingston was a computer expert at the Oakdale College Natural History Museum. Now she was sitting on top of a white piano. Her eyes were half-closed, and she had a dreamy look on her face. She was singing a sad song, swinging her stocking-clad legs in time to the music. On her fancy gown was a name tag with "Sylvia Carmichael, Nightclub Singer" printed on it. Occasionally, she would nod at the piano player.

It's a shame dogs can't applaud, Wishbone thought.

He sniffed. The man happily pounding away at the piano keys was Horace Zimmerman. He wore a bright green military uniform. There were lots of medals hanging from the breast pocket.

"Can you read Mr. Zimmerman's name tag?" Sam asked.

Joe squinted and replied, "It's . . . uh . . . 'Count Petrov Zorsky.' I hope I pronounced it right!"

Like all the other adults, Horace seemed to be having a great time. Over his eye, he wore a monocle—a single eyeglass attached to a thin strip of leather—and he laughed when it popped out of place. He replaced it quickly and easily, then continued to play the piano.

Wishbone ducked back next to Joe as a laughing Mr. Pruitt strode down the aisle. "Gee, Mr. Pruitt," Sam said. "You look really great in that outfit."

Mr. Pruitt paused long enough to kiss her gloved hand. He said, "You should remember my name, dear Lady Victoria. I am Laslo Carbine, remember? A lovely evening to you, Lady Victoria." Then he went on his way. He wore a white dinner jacket and sported a mysterious-looking black eye patch.

"What was that name?" John asked. "I didn't see his name tag."

"He's the mysterious Laslo Carbine," Sam said. "International arms dealer and master spy."

David looked at her. "How did you know that?"

"I asked him earlier," Sam replied.

"You didn't wait for us?" Joe asked.

Sam shook her head. "How are we supposed to win the game if we don't ask questions? And besides, just look at him."

Wishbone watched Mr. Pruitt stop to talk to

different people. He grinned wickedly at everyone. He seemed to have a wonderful time overacting. He paused next to "Sylvia Carmichael," and Maddy Kingston glared at him. He gave a heartless laugh and went on. *For such a nice guy,* Wishbone thought, *Mr. Pruitt really enjoys having a chance to be scary.*

Joe smiled and whispered to his friends. "I'll bet your Mr. Carbine is the one who's going to get killed."

Sam frowned. "What makes you think it's going to be Laslo?"

Joe told her, "Asking questions is only *one* way to get answers, Your Ladyship. As the great detective Hercule Poirot would say, there are other ways. You've also got to use your eyes. And you have to think with your little gray cells."

"Okay," David said. "I'm using my eyes. All I see is a lot of adults pretending to be other people."

Wishbone tilted his head. "I agree with David, Joe. What do you mean, exactly?"

Joe nudged his friend. "Come on, David. Look at what's happening. Mr. Pruitt . . . er . . . Laslo is the only character who is talking to everyone. Watch how they look at their script notes after he walks away. See? He's just finished talking to the count, Mr. Zimmerman, and now he's walking away."

"And the count is taking his script notes out of his uniform pocket!" Sam said. "Just like you said he would!"

"The count sure doesn't seem to like Mr. Carbine very much," John observed. "He's shaking his fist at him. I'll get a picture of that." He raised his camera, pressed the shutter button, and the flash went off.

"That's pretty good detective work, kids," whispered

a gruff voice behind them. They turned and stared into the face of Travis Del Rio. The sporting-goods store owner wore a broad-brimmed gray felt hat. It was the type called a fedora, with a turned-down brim. He also had on an old gray trenchcoat. He smiled at Joe and snapped a business card out of his pocket. He handed it to Joe. "Yeah, buddy, let me know if you have any more . . . brilliant deductions. I just might have some work for you." He smiled, then walked off.

Sam, John, and David crowded around Joe as he stared at the card. Joe read it aloud: "Lew Black— Private Detective."

Wishbone watched as Travis walked out of the buffet-lounge car. "Private detective! Well, he won't beat us, right, Joe? After all, you have a private dogtective on your side! Beware, evildoers! Borshoi is ready for you! Borshoi the wolfhound, Private Nose— that's me!"

At eight o'clock, Mr. Cooper, the conductor, announced that dinner would be served shortly. He said that generally meals were served in the dining car, but this evening was an exception. Mr. Cooper brought in several rolling service carts with dinner plates and beverages. Joe was still observing Laslo Carbine closely. He wondered if the mysterious man was going to be the victim—or the killer. He, John, and David shared a small table in the buffet-lounge car. Sam and her dad were at the table next to them. Joe looked around. There were only fourteen people eating dinner, so it wasn't too crowded. Joe noticed the Pattersons were not with the group.

Most people dining in the car seemed to be enjoying their dinner. The food was probably very good. However, Joe hardly noticed the meal. He was too busy thinking about his next step, plotting his next move. His script instructions had told him to be at a certain place at nine o'clock. He had a feeling that something would happen then—something big.

Whatever it was, Michael O'Hara reflected, Borshoi would accompany him with a well-fed stomach. Wishbone had his own silver dinner tray. He gobbled down a big helping of what seemed to be gourmet dog food. Wishbone licked his chops and looked very satisfied.

Joe and Wishbone wandered through some of the forward cars—Pullmans, dining, baggage. Then they made their way back again, retracing their steps.

Back in the buffet-lounge car, Joe looked out the windows. Outside, a deep, dark night had fallen. Joe felt as if the train were traveling through an endless tunnel, with no light except for what came from within the train itself. Joe wondered where David, Sam, and John were. He thought their script instructions probably told them to be in a special place at nine, too. He took out an old-fashioned pocket watch from his short pants and checked the time.

"It's almost nine, Wish—— I mean Borshoi," he said softly. "And this is where we're supposed to stand, right near the back door of the buffet-lounge car. Now what?"

The train rattled into a real tunnel, and its rumbling was suddenly very loud. Wishbone pressed against Joe's leg. Joe guessed that the dog's sensitive ears were bothered by the almost deafening roar.

Suddenly, a flash went off, and all the lights in the buffet-lounge flickered and then went out. In the sudden dark, Joe heard a loud, dramatic, theatrical-style scream. Then there was a lot of shouting and bumping around by other passengers. "Come on!" Joe said to Wishbone, groping his way forward in the car.

He bumped into someone. Then he banged into someone else. There was great confusion and a lot of muttered conversation going on. Hours seemed to go by, when, in fact, only minutes had passed. The train finally left the tunnel. A faint moonlight that had come out from behind clouds let Joe see shadowy shapes of people in front of him. Suddenly, the lights in the car flickered back on.

Almost immediately, Maddy Kingston's Sylvia Carmichael character screamed. She pretended to faint dead away into the grasp of Travis del Rio's Lew Black character. Joe smiled when he noticed that she'd looked behind her first to make sure he was there to catch her.

"Good catch, Lew," Ellen said, as Travis struggled to keep from dropping the fainting victim, who giggled.

John made his way through the crowd toward Joe.

Joe turned to John. "What happened in the dark? Who screamed?"

"Oh, my goodness, ladies and gentlemen! We've got a coldblooded murder on our hands!" Travis held the fainting victim in one arm. With his free hand, he pointed. Everyone in the dining car gasped with a great dramatic flair.

There, hanging limp and lifeless over a service cart, was the body of Laslo Carbine, international arms dealer and master spy.

"All right! Nobody leaves this car!" Lew Black shouted. He eased the fainting victim into a chair and asked a passenger to get her a cold glass of water. Then he stood solidly in the middle of the car. "I am ordering everyone to stay exactly where you are! I repeat—there's been a murder!"

The crowd gasped again. Joe had to fight to keep a grin from breaking out across his face. It was almost as if everyone had rehearsed for this moment of high drama. Joe heard Wishbone sniffing, and he looked down. The Jack Russell terrier was practically standing on tiptoes. Joe picked him up so he could see the action.

"I'm Lew Black, a private detective," Travis announced. He flashed a silver badge inside a black-leather card case. He waved Mr. Gurney over. "I believe that you, sir, are a medical doctor. We need your expert assistance, immediately."

"I'm a doctor . . . ? Oh, yes, yes, of course I am!" Mr. Gurney quickly picked up the black doctor's bag that had been on the floor next to his dining table. "I'm Dr. Mortimer Stitcher, at your service, sir!"

"Then, Dr. Stitcher, we need you to examine the corpse of this poor man!"

Dr. Stitcher hurried over to where the murder victim lay across the serving cart. He busied himself around the corpse, at first trying to find any sign of a pulse. Then he opened his doctor's bag and looked at some notes taped inside the top—his script sheets.

"It is my expert medical opinion that this unfortunate man died of stab wounds! Many of them! Too many to count! Shocking—very shocking!"

"You're adding too much to your part, Kilgore," grumbled Dr. Quarrel, coming up behind him.

"I'm doing no such thing! You're just upset because I got the best part, after all. And the name is Mortimer—*Dr.* Mortimer Stitcher—you grave robber!"

Lew Black stepped smoothly in between the two old friends. "Why don't you two gentlemen remove the body?"

The two elderly men began to push the wheeled serving cart with Laslo Carbine draped across it to the next car up. As the table creaked past Joe, the victim winked up at him.

"Look around," Joe said. "Remember where everyone is."

"Why?" John asked.

Joe began to make notes in his notebook, using his special reporter's fountain pen. "Because," he told the young photographer, "that's how we're going to solve this murder—before Lew Black does, and before anyone else does. Right?"

"Right," John said. He snapped a quick photo of the scene.

Joe looked around uncertainly. Just then, Sam walked over to the group. Then she and David gazed up and down the car. Joe had a sudden thought. The original plan was for them to work on this murder case as a team. But maybe that wasn't going to happen.

What if Sam, or David, or even John *couldn't* be part of the team?

What if one of his friends was the murderer? . . .

Chapter Five

Wishbone thought, *This is interesting! This is different! This is . . . wrong.* He puzzled over that last thought. What was wrong? *Something*—he was sure of that. Somehow, something just smelled wrong. It was nothing he could put a paw on. Still, Wishbone sensed that somehow the murder-mystery game just wasn't going the way it had been planned. *Now's the time to prove yourself,* Wishbone thought. *Little do the others suspect that Borshoi the wolfhound is, in reality . . . Dogtective Wishbone, Private Nose! I can detect with the best of them! If I can only prove that to Joe!*

Wishbone took some deep sniffs. The people in the buffet-lounge car smelled funny because of their costumes. Wishbone could smell the sharp scent of mothballs from clothing kept in storage for a long time. Traces of perfume and cologne floated in the air. He could also smell the aroma of human excitement. *Maybe that's it,* he thought. Most of these people just smell as if they're having fun. But *someone* is nervous. I mean, *really* nervous! In fact, someone here smells like a cat at a dog show!

Wishbone sat and scratched his chin thoughtfully. It seemed odd to him that a make-believe criminal would be so nervous. After all, the mystery train ride was only a game. But what if someone had a *real* secret? What if something *really* serious were happening? Maybe something dangerous?

Slipping silently through the crowd, Wishbone kept his ears on high alert. He heard little bits of conversation as the people played their roles: "Well, of course it's terrible that poor Mr. Carbine was stabbed!" "I don't think he will be missed." "It's my medical opinion that he was attacked while the car was dark." "Oh, who cares about your medical opinion, Kilgore! What about our chess game?"

Wishbone could not find the source of the strange smell. Someone in the car—at *least* one person, and maybe more—was very tense. He or she was really nervous, even afraid. But so many people were moving around that it was impossible for the dogtective to zero in on any subject.

Wishbone gave himself a good shake. "Oh, this situation is as irritating as a cat! My nose knows something is wrong—but it doesn't know *what!* Well, onward and smellward! The Private Nose will find out just what the nose knows—if I know my nose!"

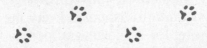

Joe said, "All right. I don't think anyone could accuse us of committing the murder. Right, everyone?"

He looked at his three friends, wondering if he could trust these new characters. After all, anyone could be the murderer!

"I was busy taking pictures," John said, holding up his camera. "It couldn't have been me."

Raising an eyebrow, Sam said, "I hardly think anyone would accuse me, sir. I am a lady and an heiress, you know."

David grinned. "You're getting really good at this game, Sam. I don't have an alibi, but I was sitting too far away from Laslo to attack him. I think we should work together. Now, our job is to— What is it, Joe? What are you looking for?"

Joe looked around, wondering what had happened to his dog. "Where's Wishbone?" He caught himself. He had to remember the roles he and Wishbone were playing. He coughed and said, "Uh . . . I mean, where's Borshoi? He was here just a second ago."

"Uh-oh," John said, looking around. "Maybe he was kidnapped . . . uh . . . I mean, dognapped."

"That's not likely," Joe said. "I don't think that would be part of the game. I'd better round him up, though. I'll be back soon. Meanwhile, start asking questions about the murder, okay?"

"Right," Sam said. "We'll divide up the car. David and John will take the front, and I'll talk to the people in the rear."

"Great," Joe said. He moved through the crowd, keeping an eye out for Wishbone. Everyone was talking a mile a minute. Joe asked several people if they had seen the Russian wolfhound, Borshoi, but no one had. At the back of the car, Joe saw that people were coming and going through the connecting doors. He thought maybe Wishbone had slipped through to the club car.

"Excuse me," Michael O'Hara said to Dr. Stitcher as he stepped past him. Joe pushed through the door.

The platform between the cars had a railing around it, but it was an open area. Joe hoped that Wishbone hadn't fallen off the train! But then, Wishbone was very sure-footed. Joe paused a moment. The air smelled smoky from the coal-burning steam engine. The evening was cool and dark. Lights flashed by now and then as the train wound through the countryside. From up ahead, the steam whistle gave a shrill shriek.

Joe swallowed. There was something almost . . . spooky about the empty night. Houses were scattered yellow dots of light, like a handful of stars dropped down to earth. Except for the clatter of the rails, Joe couldn't hear anything. The night was quiet except— He frowned and listened harder. Was that a bark?

Joe opened the door leading into the club car and smiled with relief. "Wishbone!" he said.

Wishbone was sitting up on his hind legs, waving his front legs in the air. He looked over his shoulder and seemed to grin. Joe looked around. He had not been in the club car yet, and it was a grand place. The car had extra-large, high windows that would give passengers great views during the day. The car was paneled in dark, polished walnut wood. Paintings hung on the far right wall. Instead of standard railroad-car seats, red-velvet sofas and wingbacked-style easy chairs were arranged along the walls. A refreshment bar was at the far left end. Behind it stood a smiling Mr. Pruitt. He had changed out of his "Laslo Carbine" outfit.

"Hi, Joe," he said. "Come on and enjoy the fun. Wishbone's been doing some tricks for us."

Margaret Bradbury, Henry Cooper, the Patterson twins, Travis Del Rio, and Horace Zimmerman sat on the sofas. "He's a very clever dog, young man," Ms. Bradbury said. As if Wishbone knew what she had said, he went over to her, and she scratched his ears. "Is Wishbone going to help you solve the mystery?" Ms. Bradbury asked.

"I hope so," Joe said.

"You're joking, Margaret," Horace Zimmerman said. "However, I've seen enough of this clever dog to know he's just the one who could solve a mystery. But a make-believe mystery may not be enough to get Wishbone's attention."

Joe sat in an empty easy chair, and Wishbone

66

trotted over to him and sat by his side. "Wishbone, you shouldn't take off like that," Joe told him.

Mr. Cooper chuckled. "Oh, he can't get into much trouble."

From behind the bar, Mr. Pruitt asked, "Want a soft drink, Joe?"

"No, thanks," Joe replied. He looked at the pictures on the wall. There were three in all—large portraits of men. Joe stood up and walked up to the paintings. He touched the frame on the left. Joe noticed it was bolted to the wall—so were the other two. The one on the left was an oil painting of an old man with long white sideburns and a moustache. He had a fierce expression. He stood at a desk and had his right hand on a globe. The middle painting was a picture of a younger man wearing a dark suit. He stood outdoors, and behind him there was an old-fashioned locomotive with billowing smoke pouring out. On the right was a painting of a dark-haired man sitting behind a desk. Visible through a large arched window on the right was a railroad yard. Diesel and steam trains rolled by.

"Who are the people in the pictures?" Joe asked, taking out his notebook.

Everyone turned to look. "The old boy on the left looks scary," said Michael Patterson.

"I don't know," his sister and fellow mystery-party organizer answered. "I think he looks sort of strong and silent."

Henry Cooper laughed. "Strong, maybe, but never silent! Joe, that old fellow on the left was General Oliver Wendell Windom. He fought in the Civil War. After the war, he founded the Windom Railroad

Company. You know, the Windom family was involved in all kinds of businesses. They had shipping lines, factories, and many other interests. But Oliver and his descendants were all railroad men."

Joe made notes in his book as Mr. Cooper spoke. *This is even better than the game,* he thought. *If I can only get him to talk about the spy story that Mr. Zimmerman mentioned before we boarded the train—* He turned a page and continued to write.

"Are the other two his descendants?" Monica Patterson asked.

"Yes," Mr. Cooper said. "The one in the middle is his son, Oliver Wendell Windom, Junior. And on the far right is Oliver Wendell Windom the Third. He was head of the company in the 1930s and 1940s."

Joe looked at the portraits again. He could see a family resemblance among the three men. Each of them had a strong nose and a square jaw. Their eyes were similar, too. Each man had sharp blue eyes, squinted into tight circles. They were different in some ways, though. General Windom's enormous white moustache hid his mouth. His son had a much neater black moustache. His grandson was clean-shaven, and he wore round black-rimmed glasses.

The train noises grew louder, and Joe turned around. Someone had just opened the door to the car. John Hancock stood in the doorway, holding his camera. "Hi, Michael," he said to Joe. "I couldn't find— Oh, there is Wishbone!"

"Come on in," Joe said. "Folks, this is my associate, Elvin Morse. He's the ace photographer at the *Chronicle.*"

Grinning, John said, "Hold it, everyone!" He

looked through the viewfinder, and the flash unit went off like a lightning bolt.

"Sit down, Elvin," Joe told John. "I'm questioning these people about General Windom and his descendants. That's him in the painting over there on the left, by the way."

Miss Patterson shook her head. "I'd hate to meet the old general on a dark night," she said with a smile. "I think Oliver the Third is sort of cute, though. He doesn't look as tough as the others."

"You'd be surprised," Mr. Cooper said. "I knew him when he was an old man. He'd never talk about himself, but he was a brave fellow."

Joe, as Michael O'Hara, made more notes in his notebook. "Why do you say that?" he asked. "What did he do that was brave?"

Mr. Cooper smiled. "What I'm telling you is real—it's not part of the game, remember? But back in the late 1930s, while traveling in Europe, Mr. Windom the

Third saw how bad the social and political situation was getting. The Nazi government was persecuting people. Some, like the Jews, were being harassed because the Nazis hated their religion. Others, like the Gypsies, were being mistreated because they were outsiders—they weren't an accepted part of the main society."

"We studied that in school," Joe said. "Did Mr. Windom help the victims of the Nazi government?"

"He certainly did, Joe," Mr. Cooper said. "And he did it at a time when it was dangerous to help those people who were outcasts. Mr. Windom came to the rescue. I don't know how much money he spent out of his own pocket so people could escape to freedom. But it was a lot."

"He could probably spare it," Mr. Patterson said. "After all, he was very rich. He was a railroad tycoon."

Joe sat back down. Wishbone had settled down, with his head on Joe's shoes. Joe looked at the third picture again. Although Oliver Windom III wore glasses and had a smile on his face, he did have something of his grandfather's fierce expression. He looked like a fighter, Joe thought.

As if reading Joe's mind, Mr. Cooper said, "The youngest Windom was a tough, good man. He arranged for many desperate people to escape from the Nazi government."

John walked behind Mr. Cooper and steadied himself in the swaying car. He took a photo of the three paintings with a wide-angle lens. Then he turned and asked, "How did he do that?"

"Yes," Joe said, his fountain pen ready. "How did he get refugees out of Germany?"

Mr. Cooper shrugged. "He had his ways. He smuggled lots of them out through the neighboring countries of Switzerland and France. Why are you so interested?"

Joe shrugged. "Well, I've never heard the story," he said. "Mr. Cooper, you were telling us about how Mr. Windom helped people escape from Germany. There must be more to the story."

"There is," Mr. Cooper said with a nod. "Usually the refugees—those are people who are forced to leave or are thrown out of a country—lost all their money, and most of their possessions. The Nazis took it from them. So Mr. Windom smuggled lots of money and personal property from Europe to America. That way, the refugees wouldn't arrive in their new country and have no money at all."

Travis Del Rio picked up a pamphlet from a side table and leafed through it. "You ought to read this, Joe," he said. "It tells about Oliver Windom the Third and his work in Europe. In fact, according to this, you're standing in a part of history."

"What?" Joe asked, wondering how a railway car could be history. Then he remembered what Mr. Zimmerman had said. "That's right! This is the car that was used to smuggle treasures out of Europe!"

"Treasures?" John asked, his eyes bright.

Mr. Cooper smiled at him. "Correct. You see, Mr. Windom bought some of his railway cars from France. They were built at a factory outside Paris. Then they had to be shipped across the Atlantic Ocean."

Travis nodded. "He only ordered special cars from that particular factory. They were all fancy club cars, like this one."

"And this is the last of club cars," Mr. Cooper added. "The very last one built."

Joe looked up from his notes and nodded. "I could tell this car was special. The wood looks expensive, and the carpet is so thick." Wishbone yawned. Joe thought he might be considering taking a nap on that thick carpet!

Mr. Cooper smiled again. "This is the Windom Traveler," he said. "Of all the club cars on the line, this was the finest. Now, Joe, what I'm telling you has nothing to do with the mystery game, and I'm not sure you want to get me started—"

"I'll take notes anyway," Joe said. "I've heard there's a mystery about this car—a real one, I mean." He didn't add what he was thinking: It would be fun to solve a pretend mystery, but it would be even better to solve a real one! "Tell us about it," he said.

With a chuckle, Mr. Cooper said, "Happy to, Joe. You see, when the Windom family traveled on its own railway, this was a private car. Only the Windoms or their guests could use it. Of course, railway passenger service began to dry up in the early 1960s because so many people began to travel by automobile and airplane. This car's been in the museum for over thirty years now. But before that, between 1939 and 1964, it was the finest private railway car on the Windom line."

Travis looked up from the pamphlet. "It was also a part of Oliver the Third's smuggling operation," he said. With a wink at Joe, he added, "Except, not all the valuables smuggled aboard ever made it to their destination. I think that's your mystery, Joe."

Miss Patterson said, "In fact, Henry was going to tell us about that when you came in, Joe."

Her brother nodded. "I'd like to hear the story," he said.

Mr. Cooper sighed and shrugged. "I wish it were a better one. Of the thirty or so cars built at that French factory, this was the last. Every one of the cars had secret compartments. For example, there is a false floor in this car. There's about six inches of space between the floor we're standing on and the real floor. Mr. Windom hid money, jewelry, and other valuables there."

"That doesn't sound like much space," Joe said.

Mr. Cooper spread his hands. "Since the hidden compartment is about ten feet wide by thirty feet long, you wind up with about one hundred and fifty cubic feet of space. And since individual pieces of jewelry are small, when the car came over from France in 1939, it carried about five million dollars' worth inside it!"

With a laugh, Mr. Patterson added, "And that was in the days when a million dollars was a lot of money!"

Travis laughed, too. "It doesn't sound bad to me even now!"

"A struggling photographer thinks it's a lot, too!" John added with a grin.

Horace Zimmerman was sitting in one of the easy chairs, listening to the conversation. His arms were folded across his chest. He tilted his head and said sadly, "But no matter how much money and jewels he was able to smuggle out of wartime Europe, Mr. Windom lost the main treasure. *The Adoration of the Magi* was stolen somewhere along the way."

"That's right," Mr. Cooper agreed, shaking his head.

Joe looked at the two men. Wishbone seemed ready to fall asleep. As the train rounded a curve, the

Jack Russell terrier stirred. "What is the Adoration?" Joe asked, writing the word down.

Mr. Zimmerman said, "You know who Rembrandt was, don't you?"

"Yes, sir," Joe said. "He was a great Dutch artist from the seventeenth century."

"His paintings hang in the finest museums all over the world," John added.

Mr. Patterson nodded. "Right. He was one of the good ones. You could look at his paintings and tell what they were supposed to be!"

Miss Patterson gave her twin a little shove. "You just don't like modern art," she said.

"Now, children . . ." Mr. Cooper murmured, as if the two mystery-party organizers were ten-year-olds. "Joe, Mr. Zimmerman is speaking of a lost Rembrandt masterpiece. It is called *The Adoration of the Magi*. It consists of three panels joined together—that's the kind of painting called a triptych. It shows the Three Wise Men visiting the Christ Child. For a long time it hung in a church. Then, in the nineteenth century, a wealthy Hungarian art collector bought it. In 1939, his descendants were forced to escape from Europe because of the Nazis' rise to power. Mr. Windom agreed to help them. This car had three cylinders underneath it. They looked like part of the brake system, but they weren't. The cylinders were designed so the three portions of the Rembrandt painting could be rolled up and hidden inside."

"I see," Joe said, adding that information to his notes. "So the paintings were supposed to come to America inside the cylinders."

"Except they never arrived," Mr. Zimmerman said

with a sigh. "Someone got to them. Everything else came through all right."

"Yes," Mr. Cooper agreed. "Mr. Windom saved the Hungarian family—their grandson now lives in New York City, by the way. Windom helped about fifty other people at the same time. He even smuggled out an artist, Louis Dupont, to the U.S.—he's the artist who painted these portraits hanging on the wall here. But he always blamed himself for the loss of *The Adoration*."

"There are photographs of it," Mr. Zimmerman said. "They are all in black-and-white, unfortunately. But no one has seen the original Rembrandt painting since 1939."

"That's a real mystery," Mr. Patterson said. "Who stole the masterpiece?"

"World War Two broke out that fall," Travis said. "In all the confusion, it might have been anyone."

"You'd think the thief would have tried to sell it," Miss Patterson said.

Mr. Cooper shrugged. "But a work of art like that is unique—there is no other painting anywhere like it. No museum would touch it because it's so easily recognizable—though an underhanded, rich private collector might pay millions of dollars for a Rembrandt. Then it would be well hidden away from public view. I think either the thief or a crooked collector has that masterpiece hanging on his wall—and he's not about to give it up!"

"What if the painting could be found by someone?" Joe asked.

In his Lew Black character, Travis said, "Then you'd be the most famous detective in the world, my friend."

"Let's find it!" John said, his voice excited. "That would be so cool!"

Mr. Cooper laughed. "Good luck!" he said. "Many people have already looked!"

Wishbone came to life when he heard the laugh. He yawned, curling his pink tongue. Then he took a deep sniff of the air. He stood up and stretched his legs.

Joe took a deep breath, too. The air in the car smelled of wood polish and the rich velvet upholstery. He thought it had another scent, too.

It smelled like history. . . .

Chapter Six

"What do you think about this murder?" Joe asked, his notebook and fountain pen at the ready. He had run into his mom as he and John were entering the buffet-lounge car from the rear doorway.

His mother looked at him in pretend surprise. "Oh, you're the reporter." Ellen slipped into her role as the author Marjory MacBride. "Well, Laslo Carbine was a terrible man!" She picked up a stack of typed papers and held them out. "The conductor found this in his compartment. It's my next book! He stole the whole manuscript!"

"He *stole* it, Miss MacBride?" John asked.

"He must have. I had it in my overnight bag," his mom said. "Would you like to hear a little of it?"

"Uh—"

"This is the most thrilling scene," his mom said. She cleared her throat and began to read in a very dramatic voice: 'Louisa was in love. She was madly in love. She was passionately in love. Love filled her from head to toe. She felt as if she breathed, drank, and ate love. What a pity handsome, daring, brave Frederick did not know how much she loved him!'"

Joe laughed. His mother was clearly enjoying her role. "Miss MacBride, where were you when the murder took place?"

"I was right here in the buffet-lounge car, not too far from that awful man," his mom confessed. "But I have an alibi! I was talking to that gossip columnist, Noreen 'Nosy' Nordecker. Just ask her. Now, let me finish reading this chapter for you—"

"Uh . . . thank you, anyway, but I have things to do," Joe said, both he and John edging away. He checked out the scene around him. Wishbone had jumped up into an empty easy chair, curled up, and was napping. Other passengers milled around, talking to one another. Most of them were doing the same thing Joe was doing—trying to discover the identity of the murderer. Of course, the actual murderer was trying to cover up his or her guilt.

Joe grinned, thinking about his mother's performance.

Joe and John met up with David and Sam and had a strategy session. They decided to divide the remaining suspects that Sam and David had not yet interviewed. Now Joe was down to his last interview—Wanda, as Noreen "Nosy" Nordecker. He spotted her by the bar and moved toward her.

"Miss Nordecker!" he called. "Could I speak to you for a moment?"

"Sure, Michael," Wanda said. "Wasn't the murder just awful? Were you close enough to see what happened?"

Joe blinked. *She suspects me!* he thought. Then he

had a second thought: *Maybe she's asking me that to make me believe* she *didn't do it!* "No. I was too far away. Besides, it was pitch-dark in the car," he said.

"Oh? Were you talking to anyone at the moment the murder took place?" Wanda asked, her eyes narrowing.

"It's hard to remember," Joe said. "I'll bet you couldn't remember exactly what you were doing when the lights went out."

Wanda put her hands on her hips. "I certainly can! Miss MacBride was telling me about her new book! It's a great love story!"

Joe made a note. Well, at least Noreen's story matched that of Miss MacBride—*if* both were telling the truth, then neither one could be the guilty party.

Joe continued in his role as the reporter. He asked a few more questions. Noreen asked him some of her own, as well.

Then Joe walked over to where Wishbone slept and woke him up. "Come on, boy," he said. "Let's go back to our compartment."

Wishbone jumped up, as alert as ever. At the doorway of the front end of the buffet-lounge car, Joe paused. An old-fashioned light switch was beside the door. It had two buttons—a top one for On, and a bottom one for Off.

"Just a second," Joe said. He walked to the other end of the car. Wishbone followed close behind. Joe got to the far door, the one opening into the club car. He looked at the bare walls beside the door. "Hmm . . . Laslo Carbine was standing right about there when he was attacked," he said thoughtfully. "That means . . ."

Wishbone looked up at him with anticipation.

"That means something important," Joe said. "Let's go, boy." Joe did some deep thinking as he and Wishbone made their way back through the buffet-lounge car. He didn't see his three other friends there, so he figured they had finished their interviews. He had asked them all to meet later back in his room. He had suggested that working out a timetable for the murder—creating a list of what everyone was doing up to the moment of the crime—would help. Maybe David, Sam, and John were already doing that.

Joe kept thinking that the mystery setup seemed familiar. He had started to read Agatha Christie's book that afternoon. The circumstances of her murder story seemed remarkably similar to the pretend mystery on the train. Could Mr. and Miss Patterson have copied Agatha Christie's book? The plot was very similar.

Agatha Christie's *Murder on the Orient Express* was about a murder on a famous train. The *Orient Express* was a luxury train—and it had its secrets. In the 1930s, all sorts of spies and other mysterious characters traveled on the *Orient Express,* whose route took it all the way from Paris, France, to Istanbul, Turkey. Agatha Christie's detective, Hercule Poirot, was not looking for spies. He was just returning home to England. He really wasn't looking for any kind of trouble. He found it, though, when an unpleasant man was mysteriously murdered aboard the train. Poirot immediately began to investigate the murder. The first thing he learned was that there were many suspects. Too many, in fact.

Joe flipped through the pages of his notebook. He had talked to several people. A few of them hated Mr. Carbine—but enough to kill him? Joe told Wishbone, "I think there are too many suspects."

Wishbone looked up and wagged his tail. His bright eyes seemed curious, as if he were asking Joe to explain.

Joe shrugged. "I mean, almost everyone seems to have hated Mr. Carbine. Just about everyone I've talked to, anyway. Except maybe Miss Nordecker and Dr. Stitcher."

Wishbone sniffed. The train began to climb a long grade. The track curved, and Joe had to steady himself as he and Wishbone walked down the corridor leading to his compartment.

"I don't know, Wishbone. Maybe not everyone's telling the truth. I wonder who we can trust." Shaking his head, Joe opened the door of their compartment. David, John, and Sam were sitting on the sofa, hunched

81

over a notebook. Sam looked up. "Hi, Joe," she said. "We're working out the timetable you suggested we make up."

Joe sat on the sofa next to David. Wishbone lay down in front of the sofa. "What have you got so far?" Joe asked.

David turned the notebook so Joe could see it. It was filled with columns of times and notes about what had happened, and when. "This is what we've put together so far. Next we're going to try to fit everyone's story into this."

Joe looked at the list. It was very thorough. The middle part of it read:

✒ About 9:05—lights go out.

✒ A few seconds later—a scream is heard. Voice sounds like Laslo Carbine's. A few seconds after that—everyone begins to scream as they realize what's happened. People bump into one another. John Kindler thinks that he, Lady Victoria, Elvin Morse, and Michael O'Hara were too far away from Laslo to have murdered him.

✒ Just after that—Colonel Aberdeen grabs Lady Victoria's arm.

✒ About 9:07—lights come on. Laslo Carbine has been murdered, and is slumped over serving cart.

There was more. Joe handed the timetable notes back to David. "You think the four of us couldn't have murdered Laslo?" he asked in mock surprise.

David raised his eyebrows. "I did look into your alibis, and the three of you are cleared. A good detective suspects everyone," he said. "Even you, O'Hara!"

John held up a snapshot. "Here's my proof that I'm innocent. I took this picture just at the moment when the lights went out."

Joe looked at it. The photo was blurry and not well lit. Lots of people were in it, but Joe couldn't recognize any of the smudgy faces. "I can't tell who's who in this," he said.

John shrugged. "I know. I sort of jumped when everything went dark, and I moved the camera when I did. The point is, I was taking a picture, not attacking Laslo Carbine."

Joe handed the picture back, but he couldn't help thinking that the photo just might have been a trick. For that matter, he couldn't be sure about Sam or David, either. All he knew for certain was that he hadn't been the murderer. And he was fairly sure it couldn't have been Borshoi!

Sam said, "I'm concerned about John Kindler, here. I asked him some questions and found out Laslo Carbine was trying to steal scientific secrets from him."

"So . . ." Joe said, narrowing his eyes at David. "We suspect you, too, John Kindler!"

"I'm innocent!" David protested with a laugh. "Anyway, what do you think of the timetable?"

Joe nodded. "This is just what I had in mind. What else have you put together?"

David took the notebook and leafed through it.

"Well, we've started to make up a list of suspects." David turned the page.

"Lots of them," Joe said as he looked at the list. "I was thinking about that a minute ago. Too many, in fact. Like in the Agatha Christie book."

Sam was scratching Wishbone's ears. "I'm starting to get worried," she said. With a sigh, she added in her British accent, "An heiress must be a tempting target for a bad guy. But who would suspect that her noble guardian could resort to violence to defend her?"

David grinned. "Sam thinks her dad—the colonel—might be guilty."

"Well," Sam said in her Lady Victoria voice, "I think Colonel Aberdeen may be the culprit. From talking to him, I learned that Laslo Carbine had plotted to steal the ownership of my family's diamond mines. It was a complicated plan, but it was just barely legal. There doesn't seem to be any way my family could fight him in court. What if my guardian, Colonel Aberdeen, killed Laslo Carbine to protect my fortune?"

Joe took out his pad. "Well, get ready for some more possibilities. I've got more people here who really hated Laslo Carbine. This crime is going to be tough to solve!"

David tapped his pen on the notebook. "Well, it wouldn't be much of a game if it were easy," he said. "That's why everyone has to have a motive."

"And if we get the right motive, we nail the killer," Sam said.

Joe took the notebook again. He read through the timetable and noticed that Sam and David had been trying to remember who was physically the closest to Laslo at the time in question. "I see you're also looking at opportunity," he said.

"What do you mean?" John asked him.

"Well," Joe explained, "according to Agatha Christie, a detective needs to look for three things to solve a crime. One is motive—a reason the criminal committed the crime. The second is opportunity— proof that the criminal *could* have done the crime. Since you're trying to find out who was close enough to Laslo, you're looking for opportunity."

"You said there were three things to look for. What's the last one?" John asked.

"Means," Joe said. "That's the method of murder. In this case, Laslo Carbine was stabbed. Someone had the knife. That was the means used. So if we find a person with a good motive who was close to Laslo, we're nearly there. The last thing is to prove that he had the knife."

"Or she," Sam said.

"Right," Joe said. "I've got an idea. John, stand up. You be Laslo."

"I'm Elvin," John protested.

"We're going to re-enact the crime," Joe said. "You stand here. I'm going to be the murderer. All right, David, time this."

David took out the pocket watch that was a part of his costume. "Ready."

"Tell me when the lights are supposed to go out," Joe said.

"Okay . . . now!"

Joe took a swift step toward John. "I'm pulling out my knife," he said, holding an imaginary blade. "I'm stabbing you."

"Aarggh!" John yelled. "Help me! Ouch!"

"And again," Joe said. "And again, because there were about a dozen wounds—"

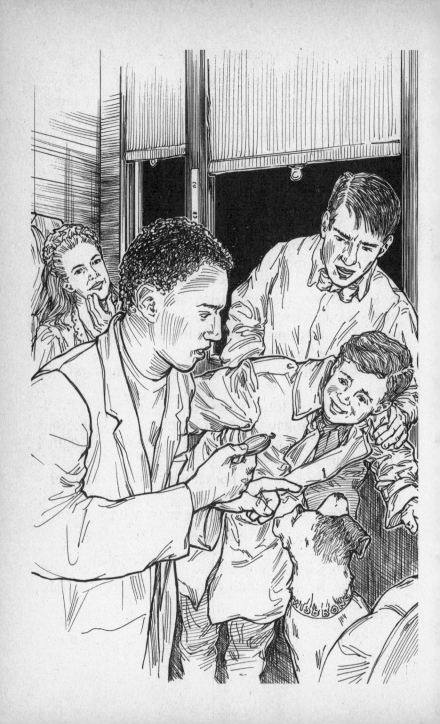

"This is wrong," David said. "You couldn't do it."

"Not enough time," Joe agreed. "Something is very funny about all this!"

"But not funny-ha-ha, though," Sam observed. "Funny-weird."

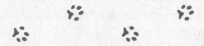

Wishbone watched the friends re-stage the murder. It was interesting—but he was beginning to feel hungry. As the kids settled down again and talked about their suspects, he scratched his ear thoughtfully. "I know what I'd like to do. I'd like to track down an after-dinner snack."

Joe said, "I keep thinking this is just like Agatha Christie's book."

Wishbone perked up. "Agatha Christie was a master mystifier! She wrote great mystery puzzles! I'm with you, Joe!"

"Look at Wishbone," Sam said, laughing. "I think he's interested in the books you read."

"Maybe," Joe said with a grin. "The *Orient Express* had a terrific dining car! That's the kind of mystery that would appeal to Wishbone—the 'What's for Lunch' mystery!"

"Tell us about the Christie book," John suggested. "How is it like our mystery game?"

Joe took a deep breath. "Well, I haven't finished reading it yet. But here's how it starts."

He began to tell his friends about the book. It had been written in 1933. The story began when Hercule Poirot, a brilliant Belgian detective, had just finished

Brad Strickland and Thomas E. Fuller

an assignment. Once the star of the Belgian police department, Poirot was now a private detective. He had been in Syria, in the Middle East, helping solve a difficult case. As the story started, Poirot was returning to England, where he lived.

Wishbone settled down and listened with his ears perked up. If he loved anything more than a good meal, it was a good story!

Joe explained that the *Orient Express* ran from Paris to Istanbul and back again. In the story, Poirot boarded the train in Istanbul. He was puzzled because the train was very crowded for a winter run. Not only that—there was a strange variety of people aboard. Poirot noticed a Russian princess and a German nurse. He met a British colonel and an American salesman. He ran into an Italian businessman and a Hungarian count and countess.

"Very similar to the types of people traveling on this train," David said with a grin. "I see what you mean."

Joe nodded. "Well, Poirot also meets a strange, rich American, Mr. Ratchett. In fact, Mr. Ratchett tries to hire Poirot. He says someone has been threatening him, and he asks Poirot to be a sort of bodyguard. But Poirot turns him down because he doesn't like something about the man."

Joe told the others that in the book, the weather got worse and worse. A blizzard hit. The train got stuck in a snowdrift on the first night. And then Mr. Ratchett was discovered murdered!

Wishbone sat up. Joe was right—all this sounded very familiar!

"Now the interesting part starts," Joe said. "It

turns out that Ratchett was involved in a terrible, brutal kidnapping and murder. And Poirot's investigation shows that almost everyone on the train had something to do with that case. *Everyone* had a motive!"

"How does it turn out?" Sam asked.

Joe grinned. "I'll let you know as soon as I finish it."

Wishbone yawned. "Well, I know how I'd like this mystery to end—with a big banquet for the detecting dog!" That didn't seem likely, so he lay down again and tried to take a nap.

Joe looked at the list of suspects he and his friends had made. They had agreed to narrow down the list, getting rid of the people who had alibis. For example, Marjory MacBride and Noreen Nordecker had agreed, when interviewed separately, that they had been talking together just before the crime took place. They could probably be taken off the list. Still, Joe thought, the situation was confusing.

"I think we need to talk to everyone on the list again," he said. "This time we'll switch names around. John, you take David's list. David, you take Sam's. Sam, here's mine. I'll talk to the people on John's list. Let's get started."

"It's getting late," Sam said. "It's past ten."

"But there's going to be a late refreshment party at eleven," David said. "No one's going to go to sleep yet."

"Except for Wishbone," Joe pointed out.

They looked down. Wishbone was sound asleep at the foot of the sofa. Sam put a finger to her lips. "We'll let Borshoi get his nap," she whispered. "Let's leave, but quietly."

For the next half-hour, Joe, David, John, and Sam wandered through the club car and the buffet-lounge car talking to people still on the suspect list. Joe, acting the role of a reporter, took notes while he had his conversations. Sam talked to most of the women. David interviewed a number of the men, including Dr. Stitcher, who had to keep referring to his own script notes. John not only talked to his suspects, but he took pictures of each of them.

A little before eleven, a bell chimed. Henry Cooper announced, "Refreshments are ready in the dining car. I hope everyone's hungry!"

Before joining the party, Joe went to his compartment and opened the door. Wishbone woke up at once, and he trotted out the door and into the corridor. Joe saw David walking toward him and called, "Let's get together for a few minutes and go over what we've found. Let's find Sam and John and meet in the dining car."

"Sure," David said. He yawned. "I like to stay up late, but there's something about this train that makes me sleepy!"

Joe had to agree. The steady rumbling and the gentle swaying of the train relaxed him, too. Still, he reminded himself, a good reporter had to keep his eyes and ears open at all times. And that went double for a good detective!

Eyes and little gray cells—Hercule Poirot would say the two were an unbeatable combination.

Chapter Seven

"**W**ow!" Joe said, awe filling his voice. "Almost everybody wanted to kill Laslo Carbine!"

Sam, John, and David nodded in agreement. The kids and Wishbone were in the dining car. The friends sat at a table in one corner. Wishbone lay under the table and snoozed. The tabletop was blanketed by stacks of notebook paper. Every page was covered with the clues they had uncovered. Outside the window, darkness rushed by as the *Zenith Condor* roared gleaming into the night.

"I don't think this motive idea is working out—at least, not like it's supposed to," Sam said.

"Okay, okay," David said, trying to sort the notes into usable stacks. "Let's be scientific about this. Maybe if we get all the motives in order, we can see some connections. We know Sam's dad . . . uh . . . Colonel Aberdeen . . . wanted to protect her diamond mines from Laslo Carbine. . . ."

"I'd say they're pretty well protected," John said. "I mean, he's dead."

David nodded. "Right, right, we know that! Okay, and we know that nearly everyone hated him. He'd done something terrible to them all." David's eyes lit up. "Hey, Joe, how did Marjory MacBride's manuscript end up in Laslo's compartment?"

"I don't know," Joe admitted. "I can't get Miss MacBride to talk to me about him. Every time I try to ask her, she just starts reading to me from her new book. Who wrote that stuff for her?"

"I know," Sam said with a smile. "I asked her to read to me, and I told her I just loved her books." She neatly added several more pages to one of the stacks. Then she lowered her voice to a whisper. "That was when she told me why Laslo Carbine might have taken the manuscript. The main character in it is based on him. It seems that Laslo Carbine had jilted her when she was a young woman. He broke her heart, and she never forgave him. Laslo wanted to keep that a secret, so he could have stolen the manuscript to keep people from finding out about it."

Joe blinked at Sam. "My mom told you that?"

Sam shook her head. "No! Marjory MacBride told Lady Victoria that. You've got to ask these questions in character, or the game won't work."

"Good going, Sam," David said, as he wrote more notes. "Of course, there's also the question of Miss MacBride's alibi."

"Nosy Nordecker didn't tell Michael that Laslo was in the process of suing her," Sam said. "She wrote a negative gossip column about Laslo. He claimed it was all based on lies, so he was suing her for libel."

"So," Joe said slowly, "maybe Nosy and Marjory

just made a deal to offer fake alibis for each other. Okay—they're both back on the list!"

Sam yawned. "I also learned that Laslo Carbine had been feeding Nosy false gossip about the movie star Mrs. Vanessa Steele, Ms. Bradbury's character. She printed it, and it was all wrong. So her job as a gossip columnist is just about ruined. Mrs. Steele is also suing Nosy and the paper she writes for. Mrs. Steele says her reputation as an actress is ruined, and she can't get any movie roles."

John shook his head. "This is very complicated. It doesn't make sense to me."

Joe shrugged. "Doesn't make any sense to me, either."

"Right." David made more notes. "That takes care of the motives for Nosy Nordecker and Vanessa Steele. And I've got two more." Joe, John, and Sam leaned toward him. "Either of you notice Maddy complaining about Laslo to several people? I pretended to be taking a nap when I overheard her."

"Oooh! Clever!" Sam whispered.

David smiled. "Thank you. Anyway, she has a great motive. Maddy's character, Sylvia Carmichael, blamed Laslo for the death of her sister!"

"Good detective work!" John said. He held up a photo. "You can add Horace Zimmerman's Count Zorsky to the list, too. Laslo Carbine cheated the Count out of a famous antique wine goblet that he had wanted for his private collection. I got that out of him while we chatted over soft drinks. He had to look at his script notes twice to make sure he was allowed to reveal the information to me."

"What about Dr. Stitcher and Professor Dire?"

David asked, looking up from his papers. "I don't think we have anything on them."

"I haven't come across anything solid," Joe admitted. "It's hard to tear them away from their never-ending chess games to ask them."

"Besides," said Sam, "they seem to be more likely to kill each other instead of someone else. Really, I've never seen two friends who liked to argue as much as they do."

"Okay, motive isn't going to help us as much as I'd hoped," Joe said. "Maybe we'll have to look for different things. *Something* should point us in the direction of who killed the miserable Mr. Carbine."

"Opportunity?" Sam suggested.

"Right!" David said, pushing his fake eyeglasses up the bridge of his nose. "Who was physically close enough to Mr. Pruitt . . . er . . . Laslo, to stab him?"

"But everyone was in the buffet-lounge car when it happened!" Sam protested. "Anyone could have done it."

David shook his head. "Nope, only someone near him would have had time to stab him multiple times."

"It had to be *two* somebodies, and maybe even more . . ." Joe said slowly.

The others looked at him, seeming confused.

"Don't you see? That's what our re-enactment showed. Someone had to turn the lights out first."

"Why couldn't it have been the murderer?" John asked.

Joe said, "Because the only light switch is way at the other end of the buffet-lounge car from where Carbine was stabbed. I noticed that earlier, and I even double-checked it."

"Cool!" John said. "I didn't think to check that out."

"I see what you mean," David said to Joe. "No one could have turned out the light and then walked through the entire car so quickly, then stabbed Laslo. The car was crowded, and it was too dark."

"So the murderer had an accomplice," Sam said, all traces of sleepiness gone from her face.

"And remember when we acted it out?" Joe said. "I was playing the part of the murderer. I pretended to stab John here, and he yelled and crumpled up. In the dark, how could I have struck him a dozen times?"

"Maybe there was more than one killer, too . . ." John said slowly.

"It's worth thinking about," Joe said to the group.

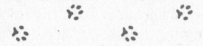

Wishbone awoke and grew even hungrier than before. There was a late supper being served in the dining car. Late suppers were his least favorite kind! He liked suppers early—and often.

The *Zenith Condor* steamed on through the night. Wishbone jumped up onto a chair to get a good view through the window. Farmlands flashed by. Wishbone could smell cows and horses. He imagined them lifting their heads as the shrill steam whistle wailed into the night air. Slowly, the farms began to vanish and more and more houses and factory buildings began to appear.

Lights began to stream by the flying train as it approached the suburbs of a large city. Still, the lonesome whistle screamed and the mighty wheels clanked down the rusty steel tracks. Finally, the sleek *Zenith Condor* glided smoothly into a blaze of light and came to a stop. In a cloud of wet, white steam, the long blue-and-yellow train came to a rest at its old platform in Centennial Station in the city of Zenith.

"Here you are, Borshoi," said a voice. Wishbone whirled around.

"Food! Wonderful food! Forget the station—this dog's got a date with a plate!" He jumped down to the floor, where Joe had set a platter of tasty meat scraps. The dog began to wade in just as he imagined a huge wolfhound might do.

At the far end of the dining car, Monica Patterson stood up and called out, "All right, everyone, we're here! The first leg of our adventure is over! We're in Zenith!" She laughed as the passengers raised their water glasses in a loud toast and cheered. "Please enjoy this fine gourmet meal, provided for us by the Windom Railroad Company and Mystery Murders, Incorporated! Tomorrow morning, bright and early, there will be special buses to take you on some shopping and sight-seeing tours of the city. I want to remind everyone to be back on time. The conductor, Mr. Cooper, informs me that the *Condor* will leave promptly at two o'clock for our special evening layover at the Windom Railroad Museum in Zenith, the permanent home of this magnificent train!"

There were more cheers. Wishbone noticed that the loudest were coming from Horace Zimmerman, antique-car collector and lover of old trains. Wishbone remembered hearing Mr. Zimmerman tell Joe about the museum. The railroad museum was supposed to be one of the finest in the country, with many displays of retired locomotives and railroad cars laid out on tracks. *Mr. Zimmerman loves trains the way I love bones,* Wishbone thought, licking his empty platter. *No wonder he's so excited!*

Monica was still talking. "And while you're having a great time in Zenith, don't forget—there is a murder to solve!"

Wishbone looked up, his expression serious. "Borshoi the Private Nose will be on the case! I'll prove to Joe that I'm just as great a detective as Hercule Poirot! I'll get right on this case—"

"Seconds, boy?" Joe said, bending over with a platter.

Wishbone licked his chops. "As I was saying, I'll get right on this case as soon as I fully energize myself with seconds!"

As Joe got up from giving Wishbone his food, he looked around. He found himself staring into the eyes of Travis Del Rio in his character of Lew Black, private detective. Lew gave him a broad wink. Joe sighed. He hoped that he, Sam, John, and David could put together the clues they needed before Travis did. He was a pretty sharp guy.

Finally, supper ended. Everyone returned to their compartments for some well-earned sleep. A yawning Joe slipped into one of the swing-down bunks in his compartment. The steady breathing above him and across the room told him David and John were already asleep. Joe sighed. He'd wanted to discuss the murder some more. Wishbone lay down beside Joe. Wishbone was the perfect partner to discuss things with.

"Solving this mystery isn't going to be as easy as I thought it would be, boy," he whispered. "Sam hit it right on the head. Almost everybody has a motive. I've been trying to remember where everyone was when Mr. Pruitt . . . uh . . . I mean Laslo . . . was murdered . . ."

Wishbone sighed with understanding, and Joe scratched his ears.

"If it was going to be easy to solve the murder, someone would have done it by now. I'll bet Hercule Poirot would know what to do! I wish I could be positive that John, David, and Sam weren't involved in the murder. The four of us—" Wishbone gently butted Joe on the arm with his head, and the boy laughed. "All right, if the *five* of us put our heads together and really examine this case logically, I *know* we can come up with the answer!"

Joe snuggled deeper into his berth.

"We're going to have to act fast if we're going to beat Travis—that Lew Black sure looks like he knows something! Maybe we need to set a trap—do something to trick the criminals into revealing themselves. Hercule Poirot used traps all the time. We need to set a pretend trap to catch a pretend murderer. I'll talk to John, David, and Sam about it in the morning. I'll bet they can come up with . . . lots of ideas . . ."

Joe fell asleep. Soon he was dreaming of murder victims in evening clothes, detectives in trenchcoats, and a lot of vaguely familiar murder suspects.

One minute Wishbone was sound asleep. The next moment, his eyes were wide open. His sensitive ears twitched. "Helllooo! What was that?"

Wishbone sat up. His head and his ears perked up. Something had happened! But what? He looked around the darkened compartment and tried to figure things out.

Okay, okay, something happened—I know *something happened. Now I just have to figure out* what *happened! Very clever dogs have* gray *cells, too—to say nothing of black and brown spots. Just gotta think. Think, think, think . . .*

What had awakened him? Then it came to him. The sleeping car had shuddered ever so slightly. *Whoa! Wait just one doggone minute! This train is* stopped, *and stopped trains don't shudder! Something really strange is going on. I can practically smell it! Wishbone, Private Nose, is on the case!*

Wishbone looked at Joe, sound asleep in his berth. *I could bark and make a lot of noise, but would that do any good? By the time the kids wake up, whatever is going on will probably be gone. This calls for direct action by the detecting dog! Scout around and report back—that's my job!*

Silently, Wishbone jumped down from the berth. He trotted to the door to the compartment. For the outside a key was needed to open it, but there was a long door handle on the inside. All he had to do was get that handle to turn and the door would swing open.

It's a good thing Joe, David, and John didn't lock the door with the key. Then I'd have to hit that little lock-button thing, and I don't really think I could.

Wishbone carefully positioned himself under the door, concentrating on the door handle. He launched himself up into the air a couple of times just to get a feel for his target. Finally, he gathered up all his strength and skill and jumped straight toward the door handle. At the last possible moment, he caught the latch in his teeth and yanked it down.

The latch turned, and Wishbone was rewarded with a quiet click as he thumped back onto the carpeted floor. Slowly, the door swung open just a crack. "Ta-dah! The clever canine comes through again! There's not a berth in the world that can hold this play-acting wolfhound!"

Success! The Private Nose comes through again! Wishbone thought, as he pushed the door open. He got it open just wide enough for him to squirm through. It swung softly closed behind him, not quite closing all the way. The corridor looked somehow different.

"*Brrrr!* Creepy! Why is it so dark?" Wishbone looked up and realized that the overhead lights were off. Only four dim night lights were on. It made the corridor look shadowy and somehow smaller than it really was. He took a deep sniff. "No one awake except me. My duty is clear. Onward!"

Then he was trotting down the corridor in a shot, just as fast as his legs could carry him. He headed toward the rear of the train.

That jolting came from this way. And now that I think about it, it was more of a bump than a shudder. Something bumped the train from behind! What would possibly run into a train? Look out, mystery, here I come!

Wishbone raced through the connecting corridors of sleeping cars. He repeated his handle trick at each connecting door. He sensed the sleeping humans in their compartments. He fought back the urge to bark. *Humans never listen to the dog, so I can't explain the situation to them.* No matter what the trouble was, he just had to find it first!

But that could mean danger, as well.

Wishbone could tell that some of the passengers were awake. He heard someone murmur sleepily, "Must have been a train on another track." No one came out of their compartment, though. He had the creepy feeling of being all alone. He reached the buffet-lounge car. All of its lights were out. The aromas of food came to him, making his stomach growl.

He was nearly to the back end of the car when the strange smell hit him. He'd been on the *Zenith Condor* long enough to learn all its major smells. This one was brand-new. It was a sharp, heavy smell, but too strange to identify. It was oily. It was overpowering. It was—what *was* that?

Wishbone's fur bristled. He was sure he had heard someone back there in the darkness behind him. He turned, his head low, his nose working hard. "This strange smell is too strong! My nose is overpowered! Well, if I have to use my eyes, I can— Yikes!"

It happened too fast. Wishbone felt a hand on his neck. Then he was snatched up off the floor. He swung in the darkness and opened his mouth to bark. At that exact moment the person holding him let go.

Wishbone fell—but only a matter of inches. He realized that he had been dropped into a sack of some kind. No! It was soft and it smelled like satin—a pillowcase!

Before he could bark, the mysterious person had knotted the pillowcase shut and tossed it. Wishbone tumbled for a heartbeat and then landed with a thump. He had fallen onto something soft. He wasn't hurt, and his nose never stopped working.

"Let me out of here!" Wishbone started to struggle and lurched against the corner of something hard. He lurched the other way and into another corner. Now that the oily smell was more distant, he smelled mothballs, and—

"I'm in a trunk!" Wishbone barked once.

At that second, the trunk lid slammed down! His bark came back to him as an echo, very loud in the closed space!

Then Wishbone felt the trunk being lifted. He was pulling at the pillowcase with his teeth. "No fair! No fair! Let me get this knot loose, and—"

Cloth slipped off his head. He had struggled out of the pillowcase. He barked once more. Then he felt the trunk suddenly being turned on its side. The clean smell of freshly laundered table linen filled Wishbone's nose. He heard a door click shut!

"Hey! Hey! I'm in here!" Wishbone barked, even though he guessed no one could hear him. He was inside a trunk, and the trunk was inside some kind of closet. With almost everyone asleep, and none of them near the car he was in, no one would be listening for a dog. Was he trapped?

Would anyone ever find him?

Chapter Eight

Joe woke up blinking. The Saturday morning sunlight slanted through the blinds of the sleeper car window. He had that split-second confusion people get when they wake up in a strange bed. Then he noticed that something else was different.

Joe sat up in his bunk and looked around. The door was slightly opened. Then, in a worried voice, he said, "Hey, David! John! Guys, wake up!"

David lay tangled in the sheets of his sofa bed. He moved a little. "Huh? What? Are we late for class . . . ?"

John, in the other swing-down bed, sat up, his brown hair rumpled. "What is it?"

Joe jumped out of his bunk and shook David's shoulder. "There's no school—we're on the train! Remember? Wishbone's gone!" Joe then opened the door wider and stepped out into the hallway—no Wishbone. He returned to the room, closing the door.

"*What?* How can he be gone?" David asked groggily. He sat up and rubbed his eyes.

John jumped down and hurriedly began to dress.

Joe was pulling on his jeans. He pointed. "The door was open! Wishbone must have done his latch trick. Help me find him. He's not supposed to be wandering through the train by himself. I promised everybody that I'd take care of him!"

As soon as the three boys were dressed, they set out in search of the missing Jack Russell terrier.

"Where should we look?" David asked.

"I know Wishbone," Joe said immediately. "We'll look where the food is."

They headed straight for the dining car. The air was thick with the smells of frying bacon and sausages and scrambled eggs and coffee. They didn't find Wishbone, but they did find Sam and her father just finishing breakfast.

"I say," Mr. Kepler began in the English accent he used as Colonel Aberdeen. He coughed. "You chaps seem—"

"Wishbone's gone!" Joe said.

Sam's eyes grew wide. *"What?"*

Mr. Kepler dropped his acting routine. "We'd better find him," he said.

"We're already looking," John told him.

"Let's help, Sam," Mr. Kepler said. "We'll search from here toward the front of the train. Boys, you go from here to the back."

Joe started to worry. He had been certain he was going to find Wishbone in the dining car.

"Where could he be?" he asked in frustration.

"Okay," said David. "If I was a little dog and wanted to get into a whole lot of trouble, where would I hide?"

John reasoned, "He's probably in one of two

105

places—either up toward the engine, or back toward the club car."

David raised his eyebrows. "Why?"

Joe shook his head. "No. Wait a minute—John's right! He's not in the dining car. The only cars ahead of it are the baggage car, the tender car, and the locomotive. He might be in the baggage car, but he can't be in the tender car or the locomotive, or we would have heard about it by now. The crew would have spotted him."

"That's true," David said.

Joe nodded. "Now, in the other direction, we have the sleeper cars. You can open the compartment doors from the inside. To open them from the outside, you've got to have a key. So, unless someone deliberately locked Wishbone in their compartment, he can't be in one of the berths!"

"If you're right," David said, "he must be toward the end of the train."

Joe was already moving. "He's got to be in the buffet-lounge or the club car! Those are the only open areas on the *Zenith Condor* other than the dining car that he could easily get into! Come on! He may be in danger!"

The three boys raced down the corridors of the sleeper cars. The names of the cars flashed past them as they ran: City of Nashville. City of Baltimore. City of Miami. Suddenly, Joe stopped dead in the center of the corridor. He was sure he had heard a faint but sharp sound. David and John almost ran into him from behind.

John asked, "Hey, Joe, why'd you stop?"

Joe raised a hand. "Listen! I know that's Wishbone! You can just barely hear him." The muffled sound of barking drifted down the corridor. In a moment, the three friends stood in front of a linen

closet at the end of the City of Miami, the car next to the buffet-lounge. It was behind the bolted door where the sound of muffled barking came from.

"Wishbone, is that you? Are you in there?" Joe asked excitedly.

The two short barking noises told Joe exactly what he needed to know.

"Hang in there, Wishbone!" Joe called as he tried to open the door. "It's locked! David, run back to the dining car and get someone to help us."

John called after David, "I know, get Mr. Cooper, the guy who runs the railroad museum! I'll bet he's got a key!"

David sped off in search of the man. Joe kept talking to Wishbone through the locked door. "We'll get you out, buddy."

When Wishbone barked again, he sounded weak.

"What's wrong with him?" John asked. "That doesn't sound like Wishbone. It's too soft."

"I don't know," Joe said, worrying. "Maybe he's sick or something."

"Maybe there's not enough air in there," John said, his expression serious.

Joe felt a sudden sense of alarm. He patted the door and said, "Hang in there, Wishbone! Help is on the way!"

Minutes passed. Joe was almost ready to try breaking the lock open. Then David led a small group of Oakdale townsfolk into the car.

"I couldn't find Mr. Cooper," David called as he ran up to the other two boys. "But I was able to get Mr. Del Rio."

"David found me," Travis said, "and together we located Margaret Bradbury. She just happened to have the spare master key." Travis inserted a little silver-colored key into the door lock. The door opened and everyone stared at the steamer trunk that filled the entire closet floor.

"Now, how in the world did he get into that?" Travis wondered. The barking from the trunk got noticeably louder.

"Wishbone is just naturally curious, I guess." Joe sighed as he reached into the closet. "And it isn't always a good thing."

Wishbone stood up on the rumpled pillowcase. He looked up from the bottom of the open trunk. "It's about time you guys got here! There's a dognapper on board!" Then, with a single bound, he jumped out of the trunk. He dashed through the startled group around him and ran toward the back of the train. He leaped up, snatched the handle with his teeth, and was through the connecting door to the buffet-lounge.

"Wishbone! No!" Joe called from behind him.

Wishbone didn't look back. "There's no time to waste, Joe! We've got a major new crime to solve this time! A *real* one! Dognapping!"

Joe ran after him. Wishbone heard Joe calling, "Wishbone! Wishbone! Oh, come on, Wishbone!"

"He doesn't seem the worse for wear," Travis Del Rio said to Joe as they ran with the others after the fleeing Jack Russell terrier.

"Mr. Del Rio, you don't know the half of it— Wishbone! You're going to get us all in trouble! Again! Wishbone!"

Wishbone sped to the end of the buffet-lounge, opened that door, then came to a stop in the last car. He turned around, sniffing. He was in the Windom Traveler, the fancy club car at the end of the *Zenith Condor*. Except—except—the smell! They were all different! And that overpowering smell was terribly strong there! *This is wrong,* he thought. *This is disorienting!*

Joe and the others came into the car. "Come on, Wishbone, quit fooling around," Joe said, bending down to grab the excited dog. But Wishbone backed away. He barked. Joe bent down, sat back on his heels, and frowned. "Something's wrong here."

"Of course something's wrong, Joe!" Wanda exclaimed as she pushed through the group, pulling Ellen along by the arm. "Wishbone is becoming a problem!"

Joe stood up. "But you know Wishbone better than that, Miss Gilmore! When he barks he usually has a good reason!"

Wishbone sniffed again. He ran in a circle and barked. "That's right. The Nose knows!"

Joe frowned. "What is it, Wishbone? What do you—" He broke off and breathed deeply. "I know what it is, Miss Gilmore. Look at how Wishbone is sniffing things around the car. That's it! It's a smell. Something smells strange in here."

Wanda shook her head. "Oh, don't be silly, Joe—it's not as if this is a real-life mystery. You're not really a detective, you know." Wanda sighed dramatically. "What's strange is that there is a barking dog in the middle of—"

"I think all of you ought to take a look at this," John said.

110

Everyone turned to him. Wishbone sat down. "Tell 'em, John! What do you see?"

John was holding a photograph. "I took this in here last night," he said. "Only look at it. See?"

Horace Zimmerman had joined the group. He looked at the photo. He stared at it. Then he looked at the paintings at the far end of the car. "I see what you mean." He looked at Joe. "See something odd?"

Joe looked from the photo to the wall. "The paintings are a little too high," he said. "Last night, the bottoms of the frames were lower, and the tops were about a foot from the ceiling. Now they're only about eight inches from the ceiling."

Travis sounded confused. "Why would someone re-hang the paintings?"

Wishbone barked again and ran toward the paintings. "Use your nose! Use your nose!"

Horace Zimmerman stepped past Wanda. He followed Wishbone to the very back of the car. Standing a foot away from the paintings, Horace sniffed the air. "This must be what Wishbone and Joe noticed. I know that smell. It's linseed oil."

Wishbone barked. "I knew that! I knew that! It's linseed oil! Yes! Linseed oil! That's what it is! Uh . . . what's linseed oil? Anyway, it's something really smelly!"

Wanda stared at her collector friend. "Oh, Horace, don't *you* start, too! Is this some part of the mystery game, or—"

Horace waved her into silence and took another deep breath. He let it out slowly and shook his head. "No game, Wanda. Can't you smell it? That's linseed oil. This car didn't smell from linseed oil yesterday, but it does today."

111

"What is all this talk about linseed oil?" Margaret Bradbury asked in an annoyed tone of voice. "And has anyone seen Henry Cooper?"

"Linseed oil is used in oil-based paints," Horace explained.

A light dawned in Joe's eyes, and Wishbone stopped barking. Wishbone ran to the wall right under the paintings. He leaped up beneath the three portraits. Then he wagged his tail and looked at Joe. "Come on, fellow detective. Get the idea! Catch on!"

Joe came close and looked at the pictures. Then he touched the middle one. He looked back at Wanda. "I don't know a lot about art. Still, I don't think that a sixty-year-old painting should still be sticky."

"What?" Wanda asked.

Joe turned. "The paint should be completely dry . . . but it's a little bit sticky." The car was getting crowded. Mr. Pruitt had just come in, and behind him was Mr. Gurney.

Horace Zimmerman touched the portrait of General Windom. "Joe's right." He looked around. "Bob, you were back here pouring soft drinks last night, so you were right in front of these. Did any of the paintings smell this way then?"

Mr. Pruitt came over and took a sniff. "No. I would have noticed."

Wishbone barked again. "Use your noses, people! There's another difference bigger than that! Much bigger! Pay attention to the detecting dog!"

Lew Black pushed his battered fedora back on his head and stood thinking. "These paintings are too large to get on and off the wall without making a lot of racket. They're bolted into the wall."

Travis grinned. "Margaret, I've got a wild hunch. Were there any other cars like this built for the Windom Railroad Company?"

Ms. Bradbury blinked in surprise. "Well, there were special club cars built for each major train that they owned—so, yes, there were a lot."

"So . . . the Windom Traveler was not the original one built for the *Zenith Condor!*" Joe pointed out. "This was the Windom family's own personal car!"

"And it was taken out of the museum especially for this trip!" Travis said. He smiled his tight Lew Black smile. "This could be the biggest clue we've hit. I have a feeling we should search this car!"

Wishbone danced around. "Yes! Yes! Come on, Joe, John, David—there's something you haven't caught on to yet!"

The club car became a whirlwind of activity as everyone began to search for clues—something to prove or disprove that the car they were in was the Windom Traveler. After a few minutes, David said, "Joe, look at this."

Joe came over. "What is it?"

David had found a small silver plaque screwed into the side of the bar. "It's got words engraved on it."

Joe knelt next to David and read aloud: "Zenith Voyager."

John leaned close. "But this car is the Windom Traveler. Isn't it?"

Wishbone turned an excited backflip. "That's right! That's it! They didn't just replace the paintings—they replaced the *whole* car! Yes! That's what they did!" Then Wishbone paused. "Uh . . . whoever *they* are."

113

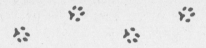

Joe found himself the center of attention. He explained what he suspected. The club cars had been switched. The car they were in was the Zenith Voyager, not the Windom Traveler. Joe asked, "Why didn't anyone notice the switch? Because they were identical!"

The group gathered around him agreed. "Is this part of the murder game?" Maddy Kingston asked Ellen. "Nothing about this was in *my* information packet."

"Not in mine, either," Ellen said. "Maybe the Pattersons know."

"This *can't* be part of the game," Joe told them.

Travis looked at him. "How do you know?"

Joe explained, "If it hadn't been for Wishbone, we wouldn't even have known that the switch had been made."

Travis looked a little worried. "Did you know anything about the switch, Margaret?"

"Me? Nothing at all, I assure you!"

Travis said, "Then that means we have to find someone who does. I think that would be either Henry Cooper or the Pattersons. I haven't seen any of them this morning. Has anyone else seen them?"

They all shook their heads. The entire group got busy with yet another search. They headed back to the passenger cars. The Pattersons' compartments were open, and empty. The beds had not been slept in, Joe noticed. In the next car, they stopped in front of Mr. Cooper's compartment. Travis knocked on the door.

Joe heard a faint moan from inside. "He's in there," he said. "Mr. Cooper!"

Again, Joe heard a soft groan.

"Stand back!" Travis said. He shoved hard against the door. Once, twice, three times he shoved—and the door flew inward with a bang.

Joe was the first one to see a figure on the floor inside. "He's been tied up!" he yelled.

"Walter," Travis said to Sam's dad, "I need some help here."

Joe watched as Travis and Mr. Kepler untied Henry Cooper and then gently lifted him onto the sofa bed. Others in the group slowly entered the compartment. Mr. Cooper moaned, *"Ohhh,* my head . . . What happened?"

"Lie still, Mr. Cooper," Ellen said. "You've got a nasty bump on the back of your head."

"We need some answers, Henry," Travis said softly.

When Joe heard that, he got his notebook ready to write in. *This is just the kind of thing a reporter like Michael O'Hara would have lived for,* Joe thought.

"I don't know what you mean," Mr. Cooper said. He rubbed his head. "Ouch! Who did this to me?"

Travis said, "To begin with, what do you know about what happened to the club car?"

Mr. Cooper raised himself, looking alarmed. "What? What happened to it?"

"The Traveler is gone," Margaret Bradbury said. "What happened to the Zenith Voyager—why has it replaced the original car?"

Henry Cooper stared at her with unfocused eyes. "But nothing's been replaced yet. We—the Pattersons and I—were planning to replace the Windom Traveler with the original Zenith Voyager—just as you requested, Margaret."

All the color disappeared from the confused Ms. Bradbury's face. "I never asked anyone to do that," she whispered softly.

Henry Cooper leaned forward, and Ellen brought him a cold compress to put on his head. "I don't understand. I got a note before the train left yesterday afternoon saying that the Windom Traveler might have a problem. I was informed that there was a small chance the car could come loose from the train. As the note asked, I arranged for the Voyager to be made ready to go. We're going to make the switch while everyone's off the train shopping or sightseeing here in Zenith."

"But the club cars have already been switched," Joe said, looking over at Travis. "They made the change last night."

"I don't understand . . ." Henry Cooper said, holding the ice pack against his head. "Everything was set for later today. Last night, I was going out to contact the city's yard crews when someone hit me from behind . . . and I woke up back here."

"But, Henry," Margaret protested. "I didn't *ask* you to switch the club cars."

"This makes no sense . . ." Mr. Cooper said. "The note is in my briefcase. It says that the crew in Oakdale thought the Traveler's coupling system—the device that connects two cars together—might not be in the best working order. It says that the Voyager could be brought in from the museum and be switched with the Traveler. And you signed the note, Margaret. You requested that we make as little fuss as possible about the problem."

"Henry, I don't know what in the world you are talking about. I never wrote or signed any such note," Margaret Bradbury told him.

"Henry, this is important," Travis said, all trace of Lew Black's character gone from his voice. "Who gave you the note?"

"Monica Patterson. Do you know where she is?"

That's a good question, Joe thought. *Come to think of it, where are both of the Pattersons?*

The twins were missing, and their compartments had not been slept in.

Joe felt goose bumps break out on his arms. Had the game of murder turned too real? Had something terrible happened to the owners of Mystery Murders, Incorporated?

117

Chapter Nine

Thinking furiously, Joe watched and listened as Henry Cooper spoke into a cellular phone: "I see. . . . Thank you very much. . . . Yes, that will be fine." He pressed a button on the phone and looked up from the table in the buffet-lounge car, where he sat. "My secretary has checked out Mystery Murders, Incorporated," he said slowly. "The address they have listed on their company's stationery turns out to be for a laundry. Their phone number has been disconnected since yesterday."

"What does that mean?" John asked, looking at Joe with a puzzled expression.

Joe thought he knew. "It means that the Patterson twins weren't who they said they were. Their disappearance has to be connected to the Windom Traveler's disappearance."

Mr. Cooper punched another number into his phone. "I'm calling the police," he said.

Joe caught David's eye. He jerked his head toward the club car. *Get Sam*, he mouthed. No one seemed to notice as Joe, Sam, David, and John slipped away—no one, thought Joe, except Wishbone, who followed. He seemed to want to stick close, Joe thought. No wonder—he probably didn't want to risk getting stuck in any more closets!

As soon as the group got to the next car, Joe said, "I think I know what's happened."

"You're ahead of me," David said.

Sam, who was in her normal outfit of jeans and sweatshirt, asked, "What is it, Joe?"

Joe glanced back toward the closed door of the car. *Good—we're alone,* he thought. Softly, he said, "Last night Mr. Cooper told me about three panels of a priceless painting that disappeared in 1939. They were on the Windom Traveler when it was shipped to the United States from France, but they never arrived."

He took a deep breath and decided to tell his friends his whole theory.

"I think those paintings are *still* hidden somewhere in the car. I think someone knew that. I think whoever changed the cars did it to be able to have time and privacy to search for the painting."

David whistled. "Any idea about who might be behind this theft?" he asked.

Joe sighed. He didn't like to make accusations— but he did, in fact, have an idea. "The Patterson twins were the ones who organized this trip," he said. "They're the ones who got the railroad museum to release the club car so we could use it. And now they're missing."

"So," Sam said slowly, "if we find the club car . . ."

"We find the Pattersons!" John finished in an excited voice. "Cool!"

"What do we do first?" David asked.

"First," Joe said firmly, "we take a look around—outside the train."

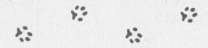

Wishbone was thrilled to get off of the train and stretch his legs! And the smells! He looked around as John, David, and Sam got off the club car of the *Zenith Condor.*

Hmm . . . he thought. *This place looks like a model-train set made for giants! Look at all these cars!* The *Zenith Condor* was on a side track, its locomotive about a hundred yards from a red-brick train station. All around were tracks, gleaming in the late morning sunshine. Red, yellow, green, black, and silver boxcars, tank cars, cattle cars, and flatbed cars were on side tracks all around.

"This way," Joe said, walking back along the track.

Wishbone padded along beside his friend. His nose, ears, and eyes took in everything around him. "Lots of train stuff here. Warehouses way over there on the left. A big tin building with a huge warped door. Over there a train creeping by—a freight train. Uh . . . why are you stopping, Joe?"

"This is the switch," Joe said, looking at a complicated arrangement of rails. "This is where the train turned off the main track to stop last night a little after eleven."

John frowned. "Wouldn't the club car have to have been taken this way, too?"

"Right," Joe said. "That means someone had to work the switch." He stared down the track bed.

Wishbone looked, too. The rails stretched far away into the distance. More switches interrupted them, with tracks curving away to the left and the right. "Wow! The Windom Traveler could be anywhere on those tracks!"

"Hey!" David said to the group, pointing back toward the train. "The police are here."

"We'd better go back," Joe said.

Outside the train, uniformed officers were speaking to some of the train passengers. Joe could tell that the Zenith police found the situation very hard to believe. They promised to be on the lookout for the missing club car and for the Patterson twins. "We'll put out an APB—an all-points bulletin—to every police officer in the city," one of the police promised.

"What should we do?" asked a worried-sounding Wanda.

The policeman shrugged. "I suppose you should go on with your plans," he suggested. "Have fun."

Joe thought that was easier said than done. A saddened group tried, though. They scattered to go shopping or sight-seeing in Zenith. Joe, David, John, and Sam went with Ellen to a park, where Wishbone played and ran. Joe didn't really have much fun. His mind was still working on the problem of the disappearing railroad car.

When everyone arrived back at the train at two o'clock, Mr. Cooper grimly said that the police had had no luck so far in their search.

121

"Do we go on with the murder-mystery game?" Joe asked.

Mr. Cooper only shrugged. "Yes. As scheduled, we'll leave shortly for the Windom Railroad Museum— it's just outside of Zenith. Tomorrow morning we'll return to Oakdale," he said, sounding discouraged.

With a shrill scream of the great locomotive's steam whistle, the mighty *Zenith Condor* once again got under way. The gleaming train rumbled forward. Joe and his friends and Wishbone sat at what had become their table in the dining car, staring out at the rail yards.

"There must be a couple of hundred cars in this place," Joe said as they slid by. "Do you think the Traveler might be out there somewhere?"

"I don't see how," Sam replied with a frown. "I mean, we got a quick look at the cars when we were off the train. They're nearly all freight and tank cars. Something all silver with yellow-and-blue trim should really stand out."

"Didn't anyone see *anything* that might help us?" John asked sadly.

Mr. Cooper sat down at the next table. "Only the yard master," he replied. "I talked to him while you and the rest of the murder-mystery group were in town."

"What's a yard master?" John asked.

Joe knew the answer to that. "It's the railroad official who makes decisions about how trains are arranged in the railway yard," he explained. "He decides which cars go to which sidings, which train gets to leave first—things like that." He put his Michael O'Hara notebook on the table and took out

122

his fountain pen from his shirt pocket. "What did he say, Mr. Cooper?"

Mr. Cooper touched his head and winced. "Not much. The Zenith Voyager arrived from the railway museum last night at ten o'clock and was directed over to a siding. The engineer running it had been hired just for the run over from the museum. Then, at ten forty-five, someone telephoned the yard master and said there was a change of plans. The cars were going to be shifted at night, instead of in the morning."

"Who was in charge of switching the cars?" David wondered.

Mr. Cooper made a sour face. "The crew that arrived with the Voyager. They had all kinds of papers and forms. My name was forged on all of them."

Joe made a note, thinking to himself that crimes were piling up one on top of the other. "What do you know about the crew?"

With a shrug, Mr. Cooper said, "They were just part-time railroad workers. They'd been hired a week ago to do the job, and they did it. And they don't know who hired them—that was handled by phone and mail. The police don't think they have anything to do with the disappearance of the car, and I agree."

Sam leaned forward. "But where did they put the Windom Traveler? Where would someone hide a whole club car?"

That, thought Joe, was the big question. A train car couldn't go just *anywhere.* It had to stay on the tracks.

So, how could someone make a whole car simply vanish?

Solve that, Joe thought, *and you solve everything!*

Joe thought the mood on the train on Saturday afternoon was different, even though Miss Gilmore and Mr. Pruitt did their best to get everyone's minds back on the murder-mystery game. People had gotten back into their costumes, but a lot of the fun had gone out of the game since the *real* mystery was on everyone's minds. Joe kept looking at his notes and occasionally scratching Wishbone behind the ears.

Who hijacked the Windom Traveler? Joe had not seen it in the rail yard. How did the thieves get away with the car? And even more important—where could they possibly have taken it? Sam had put her finger right on the heart of the matter—where could anyone hide a shiny chrome railway car? Joe shook his head.

This was a hard case to crack. In books, the writer presented all the clues, and the reader just had to put them together like a jigsaw puzzle. But this puzzle was different. All the pieces were the same color, and none of them seemed to fit. How could someone hide something like a railway car? It had to be on tracks someplace. Or could they have removed it by a flatbed truck? No, that would take too long, and it would require a crane and a huge truck. Anyway, a club car traveling on a highway would be even more obvious than a club car in a railroad yard.

"If I can just figure out how they got it out of the yard—*if* they got it out of the yard—I could figure out where they hid it . . . I *think,*" Joe told Wishbone. He sighed. "Stealing a railway car—even the great Agatha Christie never wrote about anything as weird as this!"

Joe opened his copy of *Murder on the Orient Express.* Then, for a while, he lost himself in Agatha Christie's world of fictional crime.

Joe had to shake his head in wonder as he got closer to the end of the novel—or *endings!* Agatha Christie had her detective, Hercule Poirot, solve the murder mystery *twice!* Each solution was logical, but only one was right—

What was that? Joe looked up from his book as the Condor's loud steam whistle screamed. The train was slowing down. They must be at the museum. Joe looked at his pocket watch. They had left the Zenith train station twenty minutes ago. All around stood line after line of old trains. The air brakes screeched and another shudder rumbled through the floor. Wishbone, on the seat beside Joe, sat up, his eyes wide. Outside the window, gigantic old locomotives and sleek diesels slumbered in the late afternoon light. A colorful sign welcomed them to the Windom Railroad Museum, a special overnight stop on the way back to Oakdale.

Joe closed his book and stood up. The *Zenith Condor* had returned to its home.

The schedule called for a guided tour of the museum, conducted by Henry Cooper. Joe stepped off the train and saw the conductor standing on a platform, with people already crowding around.

"Are you sure you feel up to this?" Wanda asked Mr. Cooper.

Joe saw the man nod. "It's bad enough that I lost a priceless piece of rolling stock. I'm not going to let the crooks who stole it ruin my favorite part of the whole trip! Ladies and gentlemen, I'm going to show you some of the great old trains I love!"

Joe, Sam, John, and David—with Wishbone, of course—hung back at the edge of the crowd of costumed tourists as Henry Cooper pointed out the exhibits. Joe noticed that Mr. Cooper seemed to feel a lot better. He figured that Mr. Cooper's love of trains had perked him up.

As they walked from train to train, Joe looked around. The buildings of the railway museum were huge steel-roofed sheds and a brick roundhouse. Most of the cars were outdoors in a maze of tracks, a miniature version of the Centennial Station in Zenith. Henry's voice carried strongly and enthusiastically. He stood beside a huge black locomotive with a funnel-shaped smokestack and patted its side with pride. "Now, this is the Captain Carter, a wood-burner from the Civil War era. It was built right here. Note especially the oversized drive wheels. . . ."

Joe's mind was still cranking, turning the problem over and over. *Where can you hide a train car? Where do you hide something as long as an eighteen-wheel truck? You've got to get it away from where it was because everyone is going to be looking for it there. So you take it . . . where?* Something popped into his mind, and he looked around with a jerk of his head. An idea suddenly came to him.

John, who had just snapped a picture of the Civil War train, looked at Joe. "Are you okay?"

A pleased feeling flooded through Joe. He blinked and smiled. "Where do you hide a railroad car?" he said, almost to himself.

"We've been asking ourselves that over and over, and we don't have an answer," David added.

"I think we do!" Joe said, unable to keep the excitement out of his voice. "It's *got* to be on tracks somewhere—and I don't think it's in the Centennial Station in Zenith!"

"So?" his three friends said at once.

"So, where else can it be? Well, first it's got to be someplace you can hide it—but where can you hide an entire train car? What's harder to find than a needle in a haystack?"

"What?" Sam asked, looking as if she didn't follow Joe's thinking at all.

"A piece of hay!" Joe said with a grin. "Look at all the old cars around us! There must be tons of them, and at least half are passenger cars! This is where they hid the Windom Traveler! The Pattersons had permission to move cars in and out of the museum yard! They hauled it back here! Don't you see? It's *got* to be here! It can't be anywhere else!"

And at that precise moment, Wishbone jerked his leash right out of Joe's hand. Joe whirled, saw his dog running across the tracks, and charged off after him— further into the museum rail yard.

Joe, follow me! I know you're right! If I had a ginger snap, I'd give it to you—well, I'd share it with you, anyway! Wishbone ran across the iron tracks. His leash trailed, and he ignored the frantic shouts behind him. "That's it, everyone! Sound the alarm! Get reinforcements! Those dognapping train-car stealers are out here someplace, and I'm just the dog who can find them! The Nose knows!"

He ran past a line of big boxcars, their huge sliding doors gaping open. Sounds filled his alert ears: running feet behind him, the song of the breeze in the electric wires overhead. And something else—a deep, vibrating rumble that hung in the air like a Doberman's growl.

Joe was panting from somewhere behind. "Wishbone! Wishbone! Oh, come on, boy! Wishbone! Wishbone!"

Wishbone gave Joe a quick backward glance. "Stay with me, Joe! You gave me the information I needed when you figured out the hiding place! Smells, smells—the world is a crazy mix of smells. But you have to be a dog to really appreciate them! And I smell the scent of people I know! They're here somewhere! Those Patterson twins are here!"

John was off to the side. He yelled, "Try to head Wishbone off, Sam!"

But Sam was bringing up the rear, far behind David. She yelled, "This costume wasn't made for running!"

David leaped over some rails and called, "Wishbone! Wishbone!"

Wishbone charged through a forest of gigantic spare wheels, waiting to be fitted to one of the locomotives being restored. He kept his nose low. *Both of the Pattersons were here, not long ago! They walked this way—stopped right here for a minute—then went this way!* He changed direction, leaping after an increasingly fresh scent. "Whoo-cha! Comin' through! Clear the tracks there!"

Wishbone was concentrating on the smell. He also noticed the sound. The deep rumble grew louder and louder, the heavy Doberman-like growl cutting through everything else. The low noise vibrated in the rails under Wishbone's feet.

Wishbone ran beneath a tank car and skidded to a stop, gravel flying. He looked up. A grimy, dirt-streaked car stood between two red cabooses. The car's sides were a dull, rusty-looking black. But the Nose knew! "There it is! Come on, kids! Hurry! Hurry!" Wishbone began to bark. He was still barking when Joe grabbed his leash.

Joe was gasping for breath. He felt as if he'd just played a tough basketball game. He said, "Wishbone, you know better than to run away like that!"

David stood panting next to them. "What made him do that?"

John stopped a few feet away—and he snapped a picture. *He really knows how to stay in character,* Joe thought. *He's always the photographer!* To David—and Sam, who came up shaking her head and holding her skirt up off the rail—Joe said, "I don't know what got into him."

Sam said, "I know one thing—diamond-mine heiresses don't dress well for chases!"

"Hey," Joe said, feeling strange, "look." He was staring straight ahead at what Wishbone had led them to. On a siding, a small yard engine was slowly easing a dusty, banged-up old railcar out into the yard. It was painted an ugly, rust-streaked dull black. Even the windows were so smeared with what seemed to be dust that Joe couldn't see through them. But there was something about it. . . .

"Uh . . . what's up, Joe?" David asked.

Joe pointed. "Do any of you see anything familiar about that old passenger car?"

Sam looked at it and glanced around. "Looks like any other car here—must be one of the ones they're restoring."

"No. Take a *good* look at it! Look at the lines!"

David did—and his mouth fell open in amazement.

Then John gasped. "It's our club car!"

"Quick!" Joe said urgently. "Run and get Mr. Cooper!"

Sam hitched her beautiful white dress up to her knees. "I'll go! Don't let that thing out of your sight!" She raced away.

"Hide!" Joe advised his other two friends. He looked around. "Over here!" He led John and David behind a corner of one of the cabooses. From there he peered around. A man climbed down from the yard engine and began to move a switch. Joe followed the switch and the rails with his eyes. The rails went out of the yard and onto the main tracks. He looked back.

Joe narrowed his eyes. The man wore blue-striped overalls, gloves, and an engineer's hat pulled low on his head. He wore protective goggles. Long black hair spilled from the back of the cap, and a big, droopy black moustache covered the man's mouth. Still—

The more Joe stared at the ugly black car, the more familiar it seemed. The man climbed back up into the yard engine. Joe pressed his friends back as the black car eased toward them.

Wishbone sneezed, and Joe took a deep breath. He smelled paint—fresh paint! The Windom Traveler had been disguised, he thought. They had spray-painted the car and hidden it right in front of everyone!

Joe looked around as the yard engine roared and began to roll faster. Sam was running back toward the boys. Close behind her jogged Henry Cooper, his face red. He pointed at the engine and shouted, "Vandals! Thieves! That's my club car! Stop!"

The moustached face of the engineer stared out. Joe saw the blue eyes grow round with surprise.

"That's Mr. Patterson!" Joe yelled. "He's wearing a disguise!"

With a whine, the powerful yard engine lurched forward. Joe saw that Mr. Patterson had no intention of stopping.

The engine was speeding up!

Chapter Ten

Wishbone caught Joe off guard. He jerked forward and Wishbone pulled away, his leash trailing on the ground behind him.

Wishbone glanced back. Mr. Cooper was furiously stabbing his finger at the number pad of his cellular phone. The kids and Wishbone stood watching the yard engine gain speed.

Wishbone made a quick decision. "Looks like it's up to me!" He ran after the locomotive, barking as loudly as he could. "Stop! Stop the train! Well, stop that engine and that *car,* anyway! Stop in the name of the detecting dog!"

A hundred yards ahead, a man wearing overalls came running out of a building when he heard the commotion. He stopped, stared at Wishbone and at the engine—

Behind Wishbone, Henry Cooper yelled, "Ben! Stop that engine! Throw the switch!"

Wishbone had almost caught up to the runaway club car. If only his leash wasn't dragging! "I could—

almost—jump up there—but not—with my leash!" He barked again, even louder.

With the engine only fifty feet from him, the man Mr. Cooper had called Ben grabbed a switch lever and pulled hard. Wishbone heard the rails creak as a section of them turned to the right. He saw Hank jump backward, quickly getting out of the way of the engine.

Wishbone saw the engine swerve suddenly. It turned hard to the right! Wishbone kept running straight ahead, trying to see where the train would go. Not far ahead of the engine, the tracks ended against a high mound of earth.

"Uh-oh! It's going nowhere!" Wishbone reversed his direction and ran back toward Joe and the rest—who were running toward him! "Brace yourselves! There's gonna be a—"

Cra-a-a-sshh!

Wishbone looked behind him. The engine had slammed right into the embankment. It shuddered, its wheels throwing up sparks from the rails. The club car jolted against it with a ringing clash of metal! Joe was almost there. Wishbone looked up at him. "Correction! There *was* a crash!"

"Stop them!" Mr. Cooper yelled, huffing and puffing, running up. He screamed into his cellular phone, "Get the police here right away! Someone's trying to steal a train . . . ! Yes, you heard me!"

The engine's whine stopped. Wishbone jerked his head back toward the stalled train. A man jumped from the engine, and a blond woman jumped from the club car at the same moment. They ran at full speed toward an open gate in a big chain-link fence. Through the fence, Wishbone could see an automobile in a parking lot—and he knew these two train thieves were trying to make a quick getaway.

Joe's hand was inches from Wishbone's leash when Wishbone charged again. "Come on, guys! One of those two dumped me in a pillowcase and tossed me into a trunk! I've got a score to settle! Follow me!"

Wishbone's legs pumped. His paws flew over iron rails, wooden cross-ties, and loose gravel! The two running figures ahead of him had been off to a good lead—but Wishbone was a natural-born runner. He was gaining on them.

The two fugitives sped out through the open gate only twenty feet ahead of the dog. The woman, Monica Patterson, was in the lead. Wishbone saw her jerk open a door of the car and leap behind the wheel. "No, you don't!" With his last bit of speed, Wishbone leaped ahead. The man in overalls had almost made his way to the car—

Almost, but not quite! Wishbone sped right

between his feet. The man stumbled, sprawling onto the asphalt parking lot!

Wishbone circled. "Well, well! What have we here? You *look* different, but you *smell* just like Mr. Michael Patterson! Did you have a nice trip?"

The figure on the ground pushed himself up, his railroad cap falling off. With it came a black ponytailed wig. His false moustache was dangling from the right corner of his lip. He looked wildly at Wishbone—

Wishbone heard the scream of a siren. He looked off to his left. A black-and-white police car had turned into the parking lot from the street, and now it blocked the exit. Two police officers jumped out of it.

Monica Patterson opened the door of her car. "They've got us," she said to her twin brother.

Wishbone backed away. "Correction. *I* got you! The Private Nose solves the Case of the Disoriented Express!"

Joe held on to Wishbone's leash—tightly. He watched as the police officers put handcuffs on both of the Pattersons. One of the officers came over to where Joe, John, David, Sam, and Mr. Cooper stood. "They *stole* a train?" he asked, looking very puzzled.

"Not quite," Mr. Cooper said, mopping his face with a handkerchief. "Just *part* of one."

"Why?" asked the police officer.

"I don't know," Mr. Cooper confessed.

Joe wondered if his theory was right. "I think I may know," he said. "I think they wanted the club car so they could take it apart and examine it, inch by inch. I think they believe there's something very valuable hidden in there."

Mr. Cooper looked at Joe. "Impossible," he said. "The Windom people looked in every hiding place in that car years and years ago. And they looked more than once. If anything had been hidden in it, they would have found it long before now."

"Maybe," Joe said. "But maybe not. Could we go look at the Traveler?"

Mr. Cooper looked at the police officer.

"Sure," the officer said. "Just be around when we need you. My partner's talking to someone on the radio about those two right now."

"We'll be just inside the museum," Mr. Cooper said.

"Where's everyone else?" John asked, as they headed back through the open chain-link fence.

"Having a snack in the museum restaurant," Mr. Cooper said. "They were about to go in when Sam found me. I didn't want to worry anyone, so I didn't say anything to them. I just told them to go on ahead and enjoy their refreshments. I followed Sam."

They turned a corner. Joe thought the crash might have been a lot worse. The nose of the engine was rammed a foot into the dirt bank, but the wheels still sat solidly on the rails. The club car—though its paint job made it look awful—didn't even seem to be dented.

When they got to the railcar, Joe put his hand on its side. The metal was hot, and the black paint was dry. He looked closely at the red streaks. "This isn't really rust at all," he said, pointing. "It's rust-colored paint."

Mr. Cooper ran his hand over the finish. "The Pattersons must have used an industrial paint sprayer," he said. "They could have covered the whole car in an hour or less. But why do that here?"

David said, "I was wondering the same thing. Joe . . . ?"

Joe shrugged. It was hard to explain, but he tried to put the facts in order. "Well, it's like the timetable we were working on. The Pattersons must have made up those fake orders to switch the cars. No one had any reason to think the cars *shouldn't* have been changed. So the Pattersons—or a train crew, anyway—didn't cause any suspicion when they showed up and moved the Voyager out of the museum yard. During the night, the crew switched the cars. The Pattersons then did some switching of their own."

"The paintings," Mr. Cooper said.

Joe nodded and asked, "Did the Voyager have paintings, too?"

Mr. Cooper nodded. "Yes—landscapes with trains in them, not portraits of people."

Joe felt Wishbone tug at his lease, and he held it a little tighter. "In the Traveler, the Windom portrait frames were bolted to the wall. The Zenith Voyager had landscape paintings in approximately the same spot, and the frames were also bolted. The Pattersons must have hired an artist very recently to paint a duplicate set of the Windom portraits to replace the landscape paintings in the Voyager. They were hoping no one would notice that the frames were a little higher in the Voyager, as John's photo showed. They wanted the two cars to be identical, down to the paintings."

John nodded. "But why didn't the Pattersons just

take out the real portraits and place them in the Voyager?" he asked.

"Because they wanted all the original pieces that were in the Traveler," Joe said. "They had to have everything. They were looking for a fortune, remember." He grabbed the car's handrail. "Let's see what they've done inside," he said, taking a giant step up with Wishbone to board the Traveler. The others followed.

At first, the inside of the car looked strange to Joe. That was because the light was so dim. The windows had been spray-painted, too—a dull brown speckling that looked like dust. He heard Mr. Cooper sigh in relief. "It looks the same," Joe said.

"Thank heaven," Mr. Cooper said. "They just had time to paint the outside. They didn't damage anything or make any further changes inside."

Sam asked, "Why would they bring it back here, though?"

Joe grinned. "Remember our big question? 'Where do you hide a train?' The people in the yard expected a car to come back from the *Condor* last night. They expected it to get repaired. I suppose there's a repair shed or something?"

"A bunch of them," Mr. Cooper said.

"So the Pattersons backed the car into one of the sheds, spray-painted it, and got ready to take it out again."

John snapped his fingers. "I'll bet they had more fake orders! They were supposed to take some old car someplace—except it would be the Traveler!"

Wishbone barked, and Joe laughed. He said to John, "You're a sharp photographer, *Elvin*. I'll bet

139

you're right!" Joe heard someone open the door behind him, and he turned. A tall, strongly built man had just come in. He was wearing a dark suit, and he held a leather badge holder in his hand.

"Mr. Henry Cooper?" the man said.

Mr. Cooper walked past Joe and Wishbone. "Yes?"

"I'm Agent Matthews of the FBI. We're taking into custody those two people the local police have just arrested. They're wanted under different names," the FBI man continued. "We've been hunting for them for three years. They're international thieves, specializing in stealing works of art. What we don't know is why they wanted to steal part of a train."

Mr. Cooper turned to Joe. "That was what Joe, here, was talking about."

Agent Matthews gave Joe a sharp look. "Do you have any ideas, young man?"

Joe felt butterflies fluttering in his stomach. Yes, he had an idea—but what if it proved to be wrong? That would be more than embarrassing!

He cleared his throat. "I think I may have figured it out," he said. "If I'm right—then, yes, I know why the Pattersons would steal a train car. It wasn't really the car they wanted. They were after the three-paneled painting."

"The Rembrandt painting," Mr. Cooper said. "But it isn't in the car. I've told you that."

Joe took a deep breath. It was now or never. "Not the Rembrandt painting," he said. "The paintings of the Windoms. The paintings that were on the Traveler."

Chapter Eleven

"The paintings on the Traveler?" repeated Mr. Cooper, staring blankly at Joe.

"Yes, sir," Joe replied. He spoke slowly, hoping he had figured everything out correctly. "The Pattersons had to have new portraits on the Voyager so we'd all think it was still the Traveler."

"But I would have eventually figured out it wasn't the Traveler," Mr. Cooper protested. "I'm the one who authorized the switch!"

"I think that's why you were hit on the head," Joe said. "That way, you wouldn't be around to let us know about the change. I'm not sure, but I think maybe the Pattersons were going to kidnap you—except Wishbone interrupted their plan. They tossed him in a closet, but they must have been afraid people heard him. They ran off without taking you."

Agent Matthews shook his head. "I'm getting lost here," he complained.

"We were playing a game," Joe said. "Everyone on the train was playing it." He, John, David, and Sam filled the FBI man in on the murder-mystery game. Joe finished by saying, "I think the Pattersons were going to disappear, along with Mr. Cooper. The rest of us would have been puzzled. But the Pattersons were probably counting on our thinking it was still part of the game. They needed a day or two to make a safe getaway."

"They almost got away in less time than that," Mr. Cooper snapped.

Sam said, "And nobody would have noticed those fake portraits, except that Wishbone could tell they smelled wrong—and John had a photo to prove it."

"These portraits?" asked Agent Matthews, going to the paintings. "Are they valuable?"

"Not particularly," Mr. Cooper said. "They're old, but not great art."

"They're by a French painter. . . . What was his name?" Joe asked.

"Dupont," John said promptly. "Louis Dupont. I remember."

Joe grinned at the young photographer, once more thinking that he had a very sharp assistant. "That's right. Is Louis Dupont still alive, Mr. Cooper?"

Mr. Cooper scratched his head. "I believe so. He's back in France, of course, and he's very old—"

"France?" Agent Matthews gave the group a sharp look. "The Pattersons were in France early last year."

Joe nodded. That figured. But he had one more question to ask. "You say Mr. Dupont is back in France," he told Mr. Cooper. "But he did spend some time in America, didn't he?"

"Why, yes," Mr. Cooper said, looking puzzled. "He came on the same ship that brought this railway car over in 1939. He returned home after World War Two ended and has never returned."

"Then he had time to do it," Joe said.

"To do *what?*" Agent Matthews asked.

"To take the Rembrandt painting out of its hiding place, unroll the three panels, and paint directly over them with the Windom portraits."

Mr. Cooper blinked. "Paint over . . . a Rembrandt? But why?"

Joe reached out and touched the center portrait. "To keep it in a safe place," he said. "Maybe he wanted to hide *The Adoration of the Magi* because he loved Rembrandt. Or maybe he thought he could get his hands on the painting later."

Mr. Cooper's mouth opened. It closed. Joe thought he looked stunned. "He—you mean—these panels are—under them—"

"I think," Joe said slowly, "the three panels of the Rembrandt painting are under these portraits of the Windom men."

Mr. Cooper took a long, shaky breath. "It could be . . ." he said. "Louis Dupont knew just what size each of the Rembrandt panels was. He could have painted the Windom portraits on canvases that were the same size. Then on the ship over from France in 1939, he could have duplicated those paintings directly on top of the Rembrandt panels. Dupont then probably destroyed the portrait canvases."

The group turned and stared at the three portraits. Joe heard a commotion and looked over his shoulder. Travis was leading Wanda, Ellen, and several of the other travelers into the car. "What's going on?" he asked.

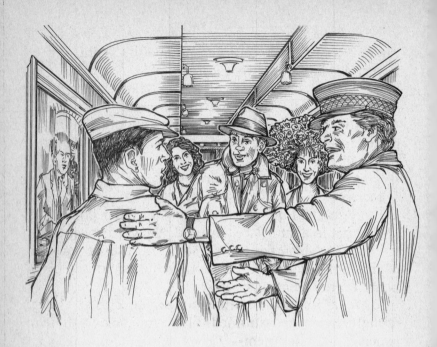

Mr. Cooper grinned at him. "You're too late, Lew Black," he said, putting his hand on Joe's shoulder. "I think young Michael O'Hara, here, has solved the crime—and not a make-believe one!"

Joe felt his cheeks burning. Everyone was looking at him.

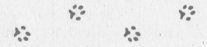

Joe had to go through his entire explanation again, though he felt almost as if he were onstage with an audience looking at him. At his feet, Wishbone looked up attentively, as if encouraging his pal. Joe finished—again—and Mr. Pruitt shook his head in wonder.

"What I want to know," Mr. Pruitt said with a frown, "is why didn't the Pattersons just go ahead and steal the three paintings on the wall? Why go through with the game and the tour?"

"They probably didn't want anyone to know that the portraits were gone," Travis said, looking at the paintings carefully. "I checked with some of the cleaning crew—the Traveler is ordinarily one of the railway museum's centerpieces. Lots of people come in and out of it every day."

"Here's another reason," Horace Zimmerman said, trying to look behind the painting of Oliver Wendell Windom III. "The frames are all bolted to the wall—very firmly bolted, too. They must have done that to keep them from swaying or falling off the wall while the train was in motion."

Joe tapped Mr. Zimmerman on the shoulder. He remembered that Mr. Zimmerman was the art expert. "Sir," he said, "is there a way to tell whether or not there are other paintings underneath these—without hurting them, I mean?"

"Indeed, there is, Joe," Mr. Zimmerman said. He took a pair of bifocal glasses out of his pocket, placed them on his nose, and continued to stare with great concentration at the paintings. "Hmm . . . right offhand, I don't see anything special about them. They seem to be pretty standard examples of 1930s portrait realism—just what you'd expect from a rather old-fashioned company like Windom Railroads. We can have them X-rayed, though. That will tell the truth."

"How about the canvas?" Joe asked. "Can you tell anything about that?"

Mr. Zimmerman looked closer. "Hmm . . . It does

look worn. There's a lot of crackling here—places where the paint has dried and tiny cracks have formed. Of course, these paintings are more than half a century old. Still, the canvas looks even older than that."

FBI agent Matthews stepped forward. "I think I can help," he said. "If you'll unbolt these paintings, I'll take one of them to our regional lab in Zenith. We'll X-ray it there, under Mr. Cooper's supervision. That should tell us what we need to know."

"Joe?" Mr. Cooper asked, smiling. "You've made the deductions. Does that seem all right to you?"

Joe felt a rush of relief. The adults were taking him seriously, after all! "Yes, sir," he said, reaching down to pet Wishbone. "It seems just fine to me!"

Wishbone trotted impatiently up and down the corridor. They were in the FBI lab in Zenith. Joe, Sam, John, and David sat on a bench against the wall. Across from them was a closed door. About a half-hour earlier, Travis del Rio and Mr. Pruitt had carried the heavy framed portrait of General Windom through that door. Wishbone sat down and scratched his ear. "I can't stand the suspense! I'd give my favorite squeaky toy to know what's going on in there. Joe, can't you tell them to hurry?"

Wishbone looked around, but Joe was going through the stack of photos that John had made of the train trip. "This picture of Wishbone is really good," Joe said.

Wishbone sighed. "Of course it is. I'm a great

146

subject for any photographer. But what are they finding out in there?"

Minutes dragged by. Wishbone got up again and moved around. Sam, David, and Joe talked about all the pictures John had snapped.

"Why didn't they ask the Pattersons about the pictures?" John asked Joe.

Wishbone looked up. "Yeah—why didn't they?"

"They're not saying much," Joe said. "They did mention that Louis Dupont told them the Rembrandt panels were still in the Traveler—but not where they were hidden."

Wishbone sat down. "Rats. But I knew they were sneaky, Joe. Anybody who would dump a dog into a pillowcase—"

"Hmm . . ." Joe said. "Look at this." He held out one of the pictures from John's stack of photos.

Wishbone jumped up onto the bench. "That? That's the one bad photo—the one that John snapped when the lights went out."

David was looking, too. "That's the picture John took just before the make-believe murder. So what? You can't see anyone's face clearly in it."

Joe pointed. "You can see this."

Wishbone peered very closely at the photo. A blurry figure seemed to be waving—at least, its hand was up in the air. "I don't get it, Joe."

"Isn't this Mr. Pruitt—uh . . . Laslo Carbine?" Sam asked, touching a figure next to the waving one.

"I think so," Joe said. "And the person with the hand in the air is just beside him."

"Who's he waving at?" David asked.

John squinted at the picture. "He's not waving," he said. "He's reaching up into a light fixture."

Wishbone blinked. "Maybe it was someone trying to change the bulb. The lights had just gone out."

Joe tapped the photo on his thumb thoughtfully. "When we get back to the train," he said, "I want to have a look at the light fixture. John, you may have come through again. I think we may have another clue here—one that would solve our make-believe murder."

"Really?" John asked. He grinned. "Cool!"

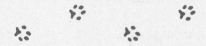

The door opposite them opened, and Joe looked up from the photo. He felt funny—his stomach was full of butterflies again. Had he done good detective work . . . or was he mistaken?

Mr. Cooper was in the lead. He held a big square of photographic paper. "Joe," he said, "I wanted you to see this. The colors are kind of off, but it gives you a general idea."

Joe caught his breath. Even though the photo had been taken with a special X-ray machine, the picture did indeed give him an idea of what lay under General Windom's portrait. The painting was of two men in richly decorated Oriental costumes kneeling and presenting gifts. Even the photo of it seemed to glow with an inner light. The painting looked very old.

"I was right!" Joe said, relaxing. "It's the Rembrandt, isn't it?"

Mr. Zimmerman clapped him on the shoulder. "Absolutely right! Joe, this is one of the panels of

Rembrandt's *Adoration,* lost to the world since before World War Two! And I'll bet dollars to doughnuts the other two panels are underneath the general's son and grandson. They've been here all along, hiding since the Windom Traveler left France in 1939 before the Nazis invaded and overran Paris."

"How much do you think they're worth, Horace?" Travis del Rio asked.

Mr. Zimmerman chuckled. "Worth? Millions of dollars."

"I think I'm going to sit down," a pale Henry Cooper said, sinking down beside Joe. "To think they've just been hanging in the Traveler all these years!"

Horace smiled and reached down to scratch Wishbone behind the ears. "And we owe it all to Joe and to Wishbone, here. If he hadn't caught on to that slight smell of linseed oil, the Pattersons would be auctioning off *The Adoration* to the highest bidders right now. We'd have never known until it was too late to do anything about it. Thanks, Joe."

Joe felt as if he were swelling with pride. "You're very welcome," he said.

After they drove in a car back to the Windom Railroad Museum, Henry Cooper displayed the X-ray photo of the Rembrandt painting to the rest of the surprised travelers. Joe enjoyed their sense of wonder and their words of praise for him and for Wishbone.

Wanda shook her head over the picture. "Isn't

this amazing, Ellen? I mean, have you ever seen anything like this before?"

With a smile, Ellen nodded. "Actually, Wanda, we have some excellent books on Rembrandt at the library."

Wanda shook her head again. "I just can't wait to get back to Oakdale and get this story into the paper! What a scoop!"

"Be sure to put in that Joe and Wishbone were the detectives who found the paintings," John said.

Joe grinned at him. "And be sure to say what a big help John Hancock was!"

John laughed. He ruffled Wishbone's ears. "Good old private-eye dog," he said.

Joe liked the way Wishbone scrunched up his eyes. He chuckled. "I think he's actually a private nose," he said.

Wishbone's eyes flew open, as if in surprise. Joe laughed, and everyone around joined in.

Chapter Twelve

Joe enjoyed all the attention at first—but then it went on and on. Mr. Cooper finally told the travelers that they had been thrown off their schedule. "Because of everything that has happened, you may just want to return to Oakdale this evening. We can have a bus come and pick up everyone if you want," he said. "Or would everyone care to spend another night on the train and go back to Oakdale Sunday morning, as previously planned?"

"The train! The train!" everyone yelled.

And so it was settled. They also agreed to get back into their costumes in the morning and continue the game. After all the excitement, Joe lay in his berth that evening and read the end of the Agatha Christie mystery again. He was grinning, because he knew a secret. He was sure the Pattersons had read this book, too—and he intended to check something out first thing in the morning!

Joe slept soundly that night, with Wishbone curled up next to him. And Wishbone, this time, did not do any late-night detecting or prowling. Very early Sunday morning, Joe rose before John and David were awake. He dressed and walked back through the train.

The Windom Traveler had been reconnected to the train. Its outside was still black and rusty-looking, but nothing had spoiled the look of the inside. The three paintings were gone, leaving light rectangles on the dark wood wall, but that was the only difference.

Remembering the photo, Joe went to the place in the buffet-lounge car where the waving figure in John's photo had been standing. He reached way up.

"Got it," he whispered with a grin. "I think I can solve the other case, too—with Wishbone's help." He went quietly back to his compartment and waited until David and John woke up. Then he suggested they have breakfast together and talk over the case.

The *Zenith Condor* pulled out onto the main tracks as the kids sat at their table in the dining car. For a little while, Joe, Sam, David, and John ate breakfast. Then Sam shook her head as she buttered a piece of toast. "It's funny to think of those valuable Rembrandt panels just hanging there all these years."

"Yeah," Joe said. "Mr. Matthews, the FBI man, says that Louis Dupont only sold part of the secret to the Pattersons. Dupont told them that the panels were in the Traveler but not where they were hidden. They're big-time crooks, I guess. They spent thousands of dollars setting this game up, just so they'd have a chance to get the Rembrandt panels."

David said, "Why didn't they just sneak in and snatch it while the car was in the museum?"

John looked up from his ham and eggs. "Because

there was too much security there," he said. "Right, Joe?"

Joe nodded. "I think you're right," he said. He didn't add that he also thought the Pattersons were aiming to cause maximum confusion. Joe believed they wanted to cover their tracks by getting everyone so puzzled that they couldn't even figure out *what* had happened, let alone *why*.

Joe slipped Wishbone a piece of bacon. "The Pattersons got back to America from France and found the Windom Traveler at the railroad museum. But they had some real problems. They knew the Rembrandt panels were somewhere in the car, but they couldn't search it. Security was tight."

"I see. Their problem was that they needed time to search," David said.

Joe nodded. "And they had to have everything that was in the car, including the Windom paintings."

"So the twins came up with the Great *Zenith Condor* Murder Game," John said. "It was all just a trick to get the club car out of the museum so they could switch it for its twin."

"And its fake portraits," Sam finished. "Boy, that was one complicated plan!"

"I guess they're complicated people," Joe agreed. *Still,* he thought privately, *it didn't pay to make things too complicated.*

Travis Del Rio came by and stopped at the kids' table. "Do you still want to go through with this?" he asked Joe.

Joe grinned. "I sure do."

David looked sharply at his friend. "Go through with what?"

153

Travis went into his Lew Black voice. "Why, solving the murder of Laslo Carbine—that's what, buddy. See, the young news hound, here, thinks he's found a clue. He wants me to gather the suspects in the buffet-lounge car after breakfast. And that means everybody!"

"Joe," Sam said slowly, narrowing her eyes, "what have you got up your sleeve?"

"Me?" Joe asked, pretending surprise. "Not a thing." He grinned and added, "Now, Michael O'Hara might have an idea or two—"

Despite his friends' laughing requests to know more, Joe didn't reveal anything else. He was enjoying the mystery too much to explain—yet, anyway.

Joe and Travis stood at one end of the buffet-lounge car—the end with the refreshment bar. Mr. Pruitt looked at them and said, "Ready?"

Joe was getting used to the uncomfortable feeling of standing up in front of a crowd. He looked at Travis, swallowed hard, and nodded. "Go ahead."

Mr. Pruitt held his hands up, and the crowd of people in the buffet-lounge car grew quiet. "Thank you," Mr. Pruitt said. "First, I'd like to thank Margaret Bradbury and Henry Cooper for letting us wrap everything up. The Windom Foundation is so pleased with the recovery of Rembrandt's triptych *The Adoration of the Magi* that it is going to match all the money raised on this fund-raising event! It's a great day for the Oakdale College Endowment Fund Foundation!"

Everyone cheered, and Margaret and Henry nodded gracefully. Then they both blinked rapidly. Joe squinted. Wanda had jumped up with a camera she had brought along, and her flash attachment was firing like a small lightning storm.

"All right," Mr. Pruitt continued. "Now, I've asked everyone who thinks he or she has a solution to the murder to write that down on these pieces of paper." He held up a glass bowl full of multicolored strips of paper. "I want to thank everyone who tried—but you're all wrong! Some of you were closer than others to the solution, but no one got everything right! However, Lew Black and Michael O'Hara have one last guess to make!"

Not a guess, Joe thought. *I'm sure I'm right—well, almost sure, anyway!*

Mr. Pruitt turned to Joe and Travis. "Gentlemen," he said, "the floor is yours."

Travis pulled his hat low over his eyes. "Listen up, you mugs," he growled theatrically. "This was one tough caper to solve, and I'm not ashamed to admit it when I need help. Michael O'Hara, here, gave it to me. Show 'em the photo, Mike."

Joe held up the picture that John had snapped. "On the night of the murder," Joe said, trying hard to keep his voice from shaking, "my friend Elvin Morse took this picture. Now, we can't see faces in it, but I noticed that someone here is reaching up. In fact, someone is reaching into the light fixture on the left there. This morning, I checked the light fixture to find out what might be inside it—and I found the murder weapon!"

Travis produced an envelope. He shook its contents

out onto the refreshment counter. Everyone stared at a big rubber knife.

"That doesn't help," Ellen protested. "Anyone could have put that there."

"Right you are, doll," said Travis in his Lew Black voice, making Ellen blush. "So Michael O'Hara and I are calling in a much better detective than we'll ever be! So here he is, fresh from solving the missing-masterpiece mystery—that famous Russian wolfhound, Borshoi! Better known to you mugs as Wishbone!"

With a bark, Wishbone trotted past everyone up to where Travis and Joe stood waiting for him.

"There's something very fishy going on here," Sam said with a frown.

"Just wait," Joe said.

"All right, partner," Travis said in his gruff Lew Black voice. "Time to blow the lid off this mystery. All the suspects—and then some—are here. Let's see who really murdered the evil Mr. Laslo Carbine!"

"Evil?" Mr. Pruitt said, acting like an injured, innocent victim. "I prefer to think of Carbine as 'misunderstood'!"

"Evil," Travis said with a grin. "Now, be quiet. You're supposed to be dead, and we're on a roll here. Sniff 'em out, Wishbone!"

Joe held the knife by its tip and let Wishbone take some really good sniffs of the rubber handle. "Who held this, boy?" he asked. "Go find them!"

Wishbone barked twice, then trotted back into the waiting crowd. People actually got out of his way as he walked by. Finally, he stopped in front of Walter Kepler, looking elegant in his Colonel Aberdeen uniform, and barked once.

Brad Strickland and Thomas E. Fuller

"I knew it was you, Dad!" Sam yelled, laughing. "I told Joe and David it was you!"

"I did it all for honor!" Mr. Kepler replied in a British accent, a big grin on his face.

"Wait, folks—there's more!" Travis called to the applauding crowd. Wishbone then stood in front of Wanda Gilmore and barked.

"It's true, it's true!" she wailed dramatically in her Nosy Nordecker voice. "That horrid little man destroyed my reputation as a newspaperwoman! Oh, the pain, the humiliation! Colonel Aberdeen and I had the crime all planned!"

"And Nosy Nordecker joins the honorable Colonel Aberdeen as one of our murderers!" Travis shouted. "But wait—there's still more!"

Next, Wishbone stopped next to Maddy Kingston, who, as Sylvia Carmichael, dramatically placed her hand on her forehead. "Yes, I killed him! The three of us passed the knife from hand to hand, each of us striking a number of stab wounds! I, Sylvia Carmichael, nightclub singer, slew him to get even for the death of my brother . . . er . . . my sister—no, my *brother!* I'm sure it was my brother! Almost sure, anyway. Oh . . . help! I've lost my script notes!"

"Wow! Three murderers!" David said, looking at John and Sam. "We thought we were being clever when we figured out there were two of them!"

"Look!" Sam whispered. "Wishbone is still walking!"

The Jack Russell terrier stopped in front of Horace Zimmerman, alias Count Zorsky, and didn't even bother to bark.

"Discovered!" The make-believe Count Zorsky clutched his chest. "He was a crook! He knew nothing of great art! He was a monster, a cur . . . Oh, sorry, Wishbone, nothing personal. Anyway, I was the one who decided we'd all do it—like the murderers of Julius Caesar, we each took a turn with the knife."

Next, Wishbone barked at Dr. Quentin Quarrel, which got a gasp of indignation from Kilgore Gurney. He turned on his friend, a grin on his face. "You old rascal! How dare you be a murderer and not tell me!"

Dr. Quarrel shrugged. "He accused me of cheating at chess."

Mr. Gurney roared with laughter. "You *do* cheat at chess!"

Dr. Quarrel threw his hands up in the air. "That's right—tell everybody."

Wishbone continued to trot around the car. This time he stopped in front of Ellen, whose Marjory MacBride character stood defiantly with her hands on her hips. "That monster Laslo stole my manuscript. I agreed to help do him in."

Wishbone looked around, shook himself, then trotted back to Joe.

Joe burst out laughing, no longer able to contain himself. "Wishbone, I mean Borshoi, identified all the murderers!"

"Not quite," said Count Zorsky. Mr. Zimmerman grinned and pointed at David. "My young friend John Kindler turned out the lights for us at just the right moment!"

"Oh, no!" David said, laughing. "I thought I'd gotten away with that—I didn't touch the knife!"

John took a deep breath. "*All* seven did it?" he asked.

"Exactly!" Travis Del Rio shouted, tossing his Lew

Black fedora into the air and laughing. "Every one of these people stabbed the miserable Mr. Carbine. . . ."

Mr. Pruitt looked hurt. "Miserable!"

Joe had to chuckle at the wounded pride in the man's voice.

"Sorry, Laslo. Count Zorsky was the ringleader, but when the lights went out, they all took a turn at murdering you." Travis laughed again as he slipped out of the old trenchcoat costume. "We will be rolling into Oakdale in two hours. Joe has earned the prize—a beautiful silver trophy in the shape of the *Zenith Condor!* Ladies and gentlemen, boys and girls, murderers and the victim, I declare the Case of the Railroad Killers closed! And I thank you!" He put his hand on Joe's shoulder.

"We couldn't have done it without help," Joe said, gripping the trophy. "John Hancock, stand up and take a bow! And Wishbone, you, too!"

The Private Nose cracks another case, Wishbone thought happily as Joe rubbed him between the ears.

"Oh, what a weekend!" Ellen gasped, almost lost in the crowd of laughing and clapping people surrounding her. "Real mysteries, staged mysteries . . . What a weekend!"

"I sure don't know what the endowment is going to do next year to top this," Wanda said, taking pictures right and left. "But I know that I'm going to be right here, just in case!"

Sam and David came over to Joe.

Joe said, "Sorry I had to keep that to myself, you two. I know we're usually a great team, but this time I couldn't trust even you!"

David winked. "Well, in my case you were right, anyway," he said, laughing.

Wishbone grinned, letting his pink tongue hang out. "I'm glad you came clean, David—the Nose knew about the knife, but the Nose couldn't know about the light switch, because who knows how many people touched it? Too many for the Nose to know one— Whoa! I'm not even sure what I just said! Anyway, pretend-it's-a-murder time is over, so now we go back to everyone being friends!" And that was just the way Wishbone preferred it.

The next afternoon, Monday, Joe and Wishbone helped John pack for his return flight home. Joe was glad that John had enjoyed his visit, and Wishbone seemed to be sorry to see his new friend leave so soon.

Ellen stood in the doorway of Joe's room and said, "John, be sure to tell your mom how much we enjoyed having you stay with us."

John laughed. "I will. And I know Mom would want me to thank you for having me—so, thanks! It was cool—I really liked it."

Ellen smiled and looked at her watch. "Are you guys ready? We've got plenty of time, but I always like to get to airports early—"

Brr-i-nng! Brr-i-nng! The ringing telephone inter-rupted Ellen.

"I'll get it in the kitchen," she said.

"Want me to carry your suitcase?" Joe asked.

"I can handle it, thanks," John said. "Come on, Wishbone!"

The three of them went downstairs just as Ellen was hanging up the phone. She looked up with a smile. "That was Mr. Zimmerman," she called to them. "He has some news about the Rembrandt painting—good news."

Joe had been wondering what would happen to the famous painting. "What is it?" he asked.

Ellen said, "Well, the rightful owner of the painting is Mr. Peter Kovak, the grandson of the man who escaped from Europe in 1939. He lives in New York, and he's a philanthropist."

Joe turned to John. "That means he gives lots of money to charity."

John grinned. "I knew that!"

With a chuckle, Ellen said, "Anyway, Mr. Kovak is very wealthy, and he has decided to have the painting sold at auction. The proceeds will go to a special charity he's setting up in memory of all the Holocaust victims. It will help descendants of the millions of people who were murdered by the Nazi government—and it will help to make sure that a similar situation never happens again."

Joe smiled at Ellen's good news. "That's terrific!" he said. "I hope Mr. Kovak knows what a big help John, here, was."

John returned Joe's smile. "It wasn't just me. Joe, you did great, too. I think you're a regular Sherlock Holmes, the way you figured out all that stuff about the painting."

Joe laughed. "Sorry, John. I'm not really Holmes. I'm just good old Dr. Watson! I know who the real Sherlock Holmes is in this family!" He laughed again as Wishbone stood up on his hind legs, almost dancing. "And here he is—black and brown spots and all!"

Wishbone was happy. He grinned up at Joe, John, and Ellen. "Sherlock Holmes? Not quite, my friends! But close—very close. I think you should just call me—" He dropped to the floor and did his best doggie bow. "Call me Sherlock Bones!"

About Brad Strickland

Brad Strickland has written or co-written more than thirty books. In the WISHBONE series, he wrote the first two The Adventures of Wishbone books, *Salty Dog* and *Be a Wolf!* Together with Thomas E. Fuller, he has also written five WISHBONE Mysteries books: *The Treasure of Skeleton Reef*, *The Riddle of the Wayward Books*, *Drive-In of Doom*, *The Disappearing Dinosaurs*, and now *Disoriented Express*.

Brad has never taken an overnight train trip like the one described in this book, but he likes trains. He was born in the small town of New Holland, Georgia, and a train yard and an old depot were not very far from his house. He remembers seeing both steam and diesel locomotives roaring through town, on their way to far-off places. The sound of a train whistle at night can still make him wonder where the passengers are headed. One of the songs he loves to sing (although off-key) is the railroad tune "The City of New Orleans."

When Brad is not writing, he is a professor of English at Gainesville College, just six miles down the railroad from the town where he was born. His hobbies include photography, amateur acting, and travel. He is married to his occasional co-writer, Barbara Strickland. They have two children, Jonathan and Amy. They also have a houseful of pets, including, at last count, an African chameleon, three ferrets, five cats, and two dogs—neither of whom has even once solved a baffling mystery!

About Thomas E. Fuller

One of Thomas E. Fuller's earliest memories was riding with his parents on the *Southern Crescent*, one of the great passenger trains that used to crisscross America. The chance to send Wishbone and his friends on one of those exciting train trips was just too good to pass up.

This is the fifth WISHBONE Mysteries book that Thomas has written with his longtime friend and collaborator, Brad Strickland. Their next joint project will be The Adventures of Wishbone *Terrier of the Lost Mines*, based on H. Rider Haggard's adventure classic, *King Solomon's Mines*.

When Thomas isn't writing for WISHBONE, he is the head writer for the Atlanta Radio Theatre Company (ARTC). His adaptation of H. G. Wells's *The Island of Dr. Moreau* won the Mark Time Silver Award for Best Science Fiction Audio of 1996. His original horror piece, *The Brides of Dracula*, won the Mark Time Special Award for Best Fantasy-Horror Audio of 1997.

Thomas and his artist-writer wife, Berta, share their cluttered blue house in Duluth, Georgia, with their four children—Edward, Anthony, John, and Christina—and entirely too many books, tapes, paintings, and manuscripts. In addition to their three cats and one goldfish, they have added two pudgy little dogs—Cookie and Rags—who wonder what all the fuss is about.

About John Hancock

John Hancock, of Northern California, won the grand prize in the WISHBONE Mysteries Series Sweepstakes. That prize was his special guest appearance in this WISHBONE Mysteries book! John was born in 1989. He is the son of John and Georgia Hancock.

John says, "I like living in California because I have a lot of friends here. We go swimming and skateboarding together, and generally just have fun." He is in the fourth grade. His best subjects in school are spelling and art. When he was asked what he would like to be when he grows up, he replied, "That's kind of hard. Maybe a millionaire!"

John says he hasn't really traveled a lot, but someday he'd like to visit Florida. He says, "I've never been on a long train trip like the one in the book, but I'd like to do that."

Explaining how he entered the contest, John told us, "I saw the contest form in a *Nickelodeon* magazine and took a chance. I knew I wouldn't win, though!" He was excited when he *did* turn out to be the winner. He says, "I was really surprised! My best friend, Cameron, was right there when I got the package that said I won. Cameron told me he was jealous, because he had forgotten to send in his form. We're both big WISHBONE fans."

John's favorite episode of the WISHBONE TV show is *A Tale in Twain*, because "I like Tom Sawyer. Wishbone did a great job in that role." Of all the WISHBONE books, John's favorite is The Adventures of Wishbone *Salty Dog*, which happens to be written by Brad Strickland. John says, "I liked the TV episode of *Salty Dog*, too. It would be neat to find a pirate treasure, the way Wishbone does in that story."

Brad Strickland and Thomas E. Fuller want to congratulate him for being a winner—and for being a wonderful character in the book, as well! John told us that he wanted to send a special greeting to two of his friends. He says, "I'd like to say 'hi' to Cameron and Jeremy—that way they can see their names in the book." And Wishbone sends John's two friends a big "Helllooo!"

John loves to read. He enjoys adventure-series books, and of course he is a big fan of WISHBONE. His favorite movies include the Indiana Jones films, especially *Raiders of the Lost Ark* and *Indiana Jones and the Temple of Doom*. He also likes to listen to alternative music. The foods he enjoys most are mashed potatoes, ham, and pizza—he'd really love to try out one of Walter Kepler's creations in Pepper Pete's Pizza Parlor!

Just like in the book, John really does have two pet guinea pigs. Chewy is the brown one. Chewy's faithful friend and companion, Moomoo, is the dark brown-and-white one. John is an athletic young man whose favorite sports include skateboarding and biking.

After his guest-starring role in this WISHBONE Mysteries book, he will probably need to get himself a few dozen pens—so he can start autographing copies of *Disoriented Express* for his many friends and fans!

WHAT HAS FOUR LEGS, A HEALTHY COAT, AND A GREAT DEAL ON MEMBERSHIP?